RUN, BOY, RUN

RUN, BOY, RUN

A novel by URI ORLEV

Translated from the Hebrew by HILLEL HALKIN

Houghton Mifflin Company Boston 2003

Walter Lorraine Books

Walter Lorraine (wl) Books

Copyright © 2003 by Uri Orlev

www.houghtonmifflinbooks.com

Library of Congress Cataloging-in-Publication Data

Orlev, Uri, 1931–
  [Ruts, yeled, ruts. English]
  Run, boy, run / by Uri Orlev ; translated by Hillel Halkin.—1st
American ed.
      p. cm.
  Summary: Based on the true story of a nine-year-old boy who escapes the
Warsaw Ghetto and must survive throughout the war in the Nazi-occupied
Polish countryside.
  ISBN 0-618-16465-0
  1. Holocaust, Jewish (1939–1945)—Poland—Warsaw—Juvenile fiction.
2. Fridman, Yoram. [1. Fridman, Yoram. 2. Holocaust, Jewish
(1939–1945)—Poland—Warsaw—Fiction. 3. Poland—History—20th
century—Fiction. 4. Survival—Fiction.] I. Halkin, Hillel, 1939– II.
Title.
  PZ7.O633Ru 2003
  [Fic]—dc21

                                                          2003001550

Printed in the United States of America
MP 10 9 8 7 6 5 4 3 2 1

Run, Boy, Run

1.

Food and Freedom

It was early morning. The streets were empty. Duvid took his little brother by the hand and said, "Come on, Srulik, let's cross to the Polish side."

"How?"

"Like the smugglers. I've seen them. They crawl through a hole in the wall in back of the house across the street."

Srulik was excited. He and his brother, who wasn't much older than him, didn't always agree. But this idea he liked.

"What's on the Polish side?"

"Food and freedom."

Srulik knew what food was.

"What's freedom?" he asked.

"That's where there's no wall and you can walk as far as you want and no one stops you," Duvid said. "Some of my friends have left the ghetto through the gate. They wait for a German soldier who looks nice and run to the Polish side."

"Did you ever do that?" Srulik asked.

"No. Going through the wall is better."

"But how do you get food on the Polish side?"

"You beg for money and buy food with it at a grocery.

1

The groceries have everything, like Pani Staniak's in Blonie before the war."

"Candy too?"

"Candy too."

Srulik was a redhead with freckles, blue eyes, and a winning smile. Even after hard times began in the early days of the German occupation of Poland in World War II, he had secretly used that smile to coax change from his father to buy candy at Pani Staniak's grocery store. But now his father had no more change.

"All right," he said. "Let's go."

"There's just one thing," his brother said. "We have to watch out for the tough Polish kids."

"What will they do to us?"

"Beat us up."

"Bad?"

"Pretty bad. Do you still want to come?"

"Yes," Srulik said without hesitating.

They ducked through the hole in the wall. Two grinning Polish boys were waiting on the other side of it.

"We'd better go back," Duvid said.

Srulik wished they didn't have to. Not just because of the candy. He missed the other thing even more, the being able to walk all you wanted, the way he could when they had had their own house in the town of Blonie.

✡

Duvid and Srulik's parents heard of the route through the wall and decided to escape from the ghetto and return to Blonie. Maybe some Polish friends there would agree to hide them. A year and a half had gone by since they were forced to leave the village. It had been a grim time.

Anything would be better than slow death from starvation in the ghetto in Warsaw. It was decided that Srulik, with his father and mother, would go first. If they made it, Duvid would follow with his older brother and sister. They would know their parents were in Blonie because they would get a postcard that said, "We haven't heard from you for ages. Drop us a line. Yacek." Yacek, Srulik's father said, was just a Polish name.

Srulik remembered the town well. They had lived there together—his parents, his uncle, his grandfather, and his four brother and sisters—in a house with one large room. His uncle and his oldest sister, Feyge, had escaped across the border to Russia when the war with Germany broke out. His grandfather was taken to the hospital one day and never came back.

Duvid guided his parents and Srulik to the opening in the wall. They said goodbye to him and crossed through it. The morning sun was already high in the sky. The streets of Warsaw looked normal. If not for an occasional German soldier, you wouldn't have known there was a war.

"Go slow," Srulik's father told them. "Make believe we're just out for a walk. Don't look at the German soldiers. Don't look at the Polish policemen. Make believe we do this every day."

Srulik couldn't resist looking at everything: the display windows of the stores, the well-dressed mothers with their baby carriages, the cars, the electric trolleys, the horse-drawn coaches—yes, the soldiers and the policemen too. His father and mother looked straight ahead. They forced themselves to behave like any two parents taking a walk with their small son. Finally, they reached the outskirts of the city.

Srulik was overjoyed. Everything made him smile: the green fields, the flowers growing by the roadside, the cows and horses grazing in the grass, the big blue sky that stretched to the horizon, where a thin black line marked the edge of the Kampinowski Forest. It was just like before the war.

Suddenly three German soldiers on motorcycles came speeding toward them. Srulik's father jumped into a ditch by the side of the road. He and his mother dived for the other side. His father got away. The Germans caught him and his mother, put them in the sidecar, and brought them to the Gestapo. His mother was given a whipping and they were returned to the ghetto.

Srulik's mother lay for a long while in bed. His father didn't return.

✡

It took two weeks for Srulik's mother to recover enough to go foraging with him again in the ghetto's garbage bins. Removing the lid from a bin, she picked him up and lowered him into it, even though he told her he could do it by himself. He even showed her how, with the help of a running start, he could grab the rim of the bin and vault over. This was easier when it was made of bricks. The metal cans were harder.

"You don't get as dirty when I help you," his mother answered.

"Mama, what difference does that make?" Srulik asked.

Still, he thought, maybe she was right.

The work demanded concentration. When his arms

4

didn't reach all the way into the garbage, he used a stick or a broken board. He looked for the peels of potatoes, carrots, beets, and apples and sometimes found old, moldy bread. Everything went into a straw basket that he handed to his mother. At home, she picked out what was edible and cooked it. Although each family received food rations, these were too small to keep them alive. And in winter, the garbage froze and was hard to handle. It was better once he found a pair of torn woolen gloves and his mother mended them for him.

Now, though, it was a hot June day and Srulik was already eight years old. The trouble with the summer was that the garbage smelled bad and the flies kept buzzing around his head. You couldn't tell them that they'd be better off looking in the garbage. It took something unusually smelly to attract their attention. There were ordinary flies and there were green bottles, which his brother Duvid called "death flies." Today nothing smelled that bad, and there was no way of keeping the flies off him.

The basket was full. "Mama?" he called, ready to hand it to her.

There was no answer. No hands took the basket. He stood up and peered out of the garbage bin. Some boys were playing soccer near the ghetto wall that cut the street in half. Srulik jumped from the bin and ran along the street, looking for his mother. For a second he thought that a woman sitting hunched on a stoop was her. But it wasn't.

He ran back to the garbage bin. Perhaps she had run away from a policeman and come back. Someone was standing there, emptying a pail of garbage. It wasn't his mother. She had vanished as though into thin air.

Srulik stood wringing his fingers, just like his mother did when she was worried or desperate. He didn't know the way home. He looked around as though in a fog. Everything was still the same. The houses and windows on both sides of the street hadn't changed. People continued to walk busily on the sidewalks. The soccer game in the empty lot was still going on. Even he, Srulik, would have looked to someone else like the same boy. Yet inside he felt as though the bottom had dropped out of himself. He pulled himself together and ran to join the boys playing by the wall.

2.

Can You Steal?

Srulik was an athletic boy with long legs. Soccer was a game he had learned to play back on a muddy field in Blonie. He and his friends had used the same kind of "ball," a tin can wrapped in rags.

There were eight boys playing. Srulik made nine. One boy volunteered to sit the game out so that Srulik could join it. Though it was hot, the boy was wearing a grown-up's tattered jacket that was too big for him and made it hard to run. After a while, the boys stopped the game and stood looking at Srulik and whispering. Then they formed a circle around him and studied him more carefully.

"He's thin enough," the biggest boy said.

"He'll fit," said someone else.

"Fit where?" Srulik asked.

"Are you hungry?" the boy in the jacket asked.

"Yes," Srulik said. He had forgotten that he was.

"Moishele," the big boy said to the boy with the jacket, "give him a piece."

Now Srulik saw that the pockets of the jacket were bulging. Moishele glanced up and down, saw that no one was watching, took out a sausage from one pocket and a pocket knife from the other, and cut a thick slab of it for

Srulik. He hadn't had such a treat in a long time.

"Stick with us," the big boy said. "When it's dark, we'll lower you through a basement window into a store that has more sausages like this one. It's too small for any of us to fit through, but you might make it. Can you steal?"

Srulik shrugged. He could steal. He could do anything for more sausage.

"I want some more," he said.

"Should I give him some, Yankel?"

"Give him some," the big boy said.

The boys went on playing until it began to get dark. Then they hid their ball underneath a pile of junk and set out on the run, darting around the pedestrians in the street. When they reached a bricked-up doorway, they stopped to wait for the night curfew to begin. From the way the streets were emptying, they knew it would be soon. Meanwhile, Moishele took out the sausage and cut a piece for everyone. When they had eaten, he took out some cigarettes and matches, cut each cigarette in half, and passed the halves out importantly. The two biggest boys each got his own cigarette.

"Do you smoke?" Moishele asked Srulik.

"No."

"You have to if you want to join the gang."

His brother Duvid had once tried getting him to take a drag on a cigarette. It was bitter and made him cough and choke.

"I'd rather not," he said.

"Leave him alone," Yankel told Moishele.

A well-dressed man passed by. One of the boys

approached him and said, "Please, mister, can you spare some change? We're hungry."

The man looked at them and snapped, "You bums! How come you have enough money for cigarettes?"

The street was soon deserted. It was time to go into action. The store they planned to break in to faced an alleyway. The window was very small.

"Start shouting," Yankel said.

All the boys began to shout as if they were fighting. Under the cover of the noise, Yankel took a stone and smashed the window. Someone looked down from a top floor and yelled, "You bums! Get out of here!"

"All right, ma'am," Moishele said.

They moved off and came back a few minutes later. Yankel stuck his hand through the window and removed the broken glass. Then Srulik was tied to a rope. He wriggled through the window and Yankel lowered him carefully.

"Hey, Red," he called softly. "Leave the rope on and coil it around you. Tell me what you see down there."

Srulik tried to make out his surroundings, but it was too dark to see anything.

"Nothing," he called up.

"Moishele," Yankel said, annoyed, "why didn't you give him a box of matches?"

"Why didn't you give him one yourself?"

A box of matches landed on the floor. Srulik groped for it, found it, and lit a match.

"Do you see any sausage?"

"No," he said. "Just bottles."

"Vodka?"

"How can you tell?"

"It says."

"I can't read."

"Pass one up through the window."

He found a chair, put it beneath the window, stood on it, and reached as high with the bottle as he could.

"Great! How many more like these are there?"

"I see two. There might be more in the closet, but it's locked."

"Look for cigarettes."

It wasn't very different from going through the garbage with his mother. But the results were better: cigarettes, matches, several bottles of vodka, and two whole sausages hidden under the counter. Yankel told him to put the cigarettes and matches in his pockets and pass up the end of the rope.

"Quick!"

Srulik was yanked upward just in the nick of time. The footsteps of the night patrol were approaching. The gang took to its heels.

The boys knew the neighborhood and the buildings that had no gatekeeper. At night they slept in empty lofts. The best lofts were the ones with old rags or discarded mattresses that they could sleep on. If they couldn't find a loft that wasn't locked, they bedded down on the stairs.

They found a loft that was open. A match scratched and a candle was lit.

"Moishele," Srulik said, "I have more matches in my pockets."

"Hold on to them," Moishele answered. "My pockets are stuffed full."

Moishele took out some bread and they sat down to eat. The menu was more sausage, bread, and water. Then they lay down to sleep. Srulik found a beat-up old mattress and dragged it over to Yankel's. One of the boys tried grabbing it from him.

"Hey, Red, that's my mattress," he said.

"Leave him alone," Yankel threatened. "It's his now."

Yankel went to a crate in the corner of the loft and pulled out the remains of an old army coat. "Here," he said to Srulik. "Use it as a blanket."

Srulik felt grateful for being taken under Yankel's wing.

"Lights out!" Moishele announced.

"One more minute . . . just a minute . . ." voices called.

"Put out the candle," Yankel said.

Moishele wet his two fingers in his mouth and snuffed out the flame. It was pitch dark.

Darkness covered the streets of the Warsaw ghetto. Since the German invasion of Russia, there was a blackout every night. In winter, when the skies were cloudy and it got dark before the curfew, people bumped into each other in the street. Someone had had the idea of coating pins with phosphorus, and whoever could afford one wore a pin that glowed in the dark. The pins came in human and animal shapes—dogs, cats, butterflies, birds, even chimney sweeps. Srulik envied whoever had one. Although he begged his father for one, there was no money. And then one day he found a butterfly pin in the garbage. The more he left in sunlight during the day, the more it shone at night. He would put it on the window sill, where it caught the sun's rays peeping over the roofs of the houses. At night it gave off a greenish glow. He could even see the tips of his fingers if he held them close to it.

It was quiet in the loft once the candle was snuffed out. They could hear the tenants of the building talking in muffled voices, the sounds of pots and dishes being washed, the creaking and banging of doors, and steps from the courtyard below. Srulik took out his shiny butterfly to push back the darkness, as he always did before falling asleep. Even after he shut his eyes, the world was less black then. There was enough light to remember and dream of all the things he had seen during the day.

"What do you have there?" Yankel asked.

"A glow pin," Srulik said.

"Let me see it."

Srulik groped for Yankel's hand and gave it to him. "I found it in some garbage."

"You did a good day's work, Srulik," Yankel said, handing it back to him.

"What will you do with the vodka?"

"Sell it." There was a moment's silence. Then Yankel asked, "How come you joined us?"

"I was looking for food in the garbage with my mother. She disappeared."

Yankel sat up. "You have a mother?" he asked wonderingly.

"Yes," Srulik said. He didn't see anything so special about it.

Word spread through the loft that the redheaded boy

had a mother. All the boys gathered around him. They wanted to hear about her. What did she look like? What did she give him to eat?

"Is she pretty?"

Srulik couldn't say what his mother looked like. He had never thought if she was pretty or not.

"Yes," he said.

"She's not dead?"

"No." He felt sure of that.

"Then where is she?"

"I guess at home."

"Then why aren't you with her?"

"I don't know how to get there."

"You don't know the name of the street?"

"No," he said sadly.

"You're not from Warsaw?"

"No. We're from Blonie."

The Warsaw Ghetto was large, not like the little ghetto in Blonie. It had tall buildings and lots of streets. His new friends, he was told, came from the countryside too. Some had been separated from their parents during their deportation to Warsaw.

"Try to think," Yankel said. "If you can remember where your house is, we'll find your mother for you."

"Where is your mother?" Srulik asked.

"She's dead. My father died too, in Warsaw."

Srulik stretched out on his mattress. He wasn't used to sleeping by himself. He would have given anything to be in one bed again with his brother Duvid, who always kicked him and pulled the blanket. He could picture their building clearly: the entrance, the rickety wooden stairs, the door of their apartment, which was never shut during the day because of all the people coming in and out. He just couldn't remember how to get there, even though he could see his mother as though she were in front of his eyes. It was weird how someone could be so close and yet so out of reach.

Before he knew it, it was morning.

✡

The biggest boys went out to sell the vodka and cigarettes and bought bread and sugar with the money. Srulik took a piece of bread, wet it, and dipped it in the sugar. The bread wasn't sliced as neatly as his mother's, but it tasted the same.

The boys brought him to their friend, Yoyneh the shoemaker, who sometimes made them tea in exchange for sugar. He was working in the doorway of the little cubbyhole that was his shoe shop.

"We have a new gang member," Yankel said, introducing Srulik.

Yoyneh glanced up at him. Srulik smiled. The shoemaker reached out a callused hand and gently took Srulik's chin.

"God has given you what not many people have, son," he said, looking first at Srulik's face and then at his shoes. "I'm too busy today, but come another time and I'll mend your shoes for you."

"He has a mother," Yankel said. "He just doesn't know where she lives."

Yoyneh frowned. Telling Srulik to sit, he asked him what his street looked like.

"Like a street," Srulik said.

14

"Do you remember the number of the house?"

"Yes. Ten."

"And the name of the street?"

"No."

"Look at that." Yoyneh pointed at a street sign. "Did you have one on your street?"

Srulik looked at the sign and shook his head in sorrow. He couldn't remember.

"I'll go to the police," Yoyneh said. "Maybe someone reported you missing. And you," he told Yankel, "should take him around the ghetto. Maybe you'll hit the right street by chance."

They finished their tea. Yankel took Srulik and they crisscrossed back and forth through the crowded streets of the ghetto. "Maybe it's this street?" Yankel asked at each corner.

"No," Srulik answered each time.

In the end they gave up and rejoined the gang.

✡

Srulik was getting used to the new way of life—sleeping in lofts, roaming the streets, shoplifting by day, and breaking into stores before the curfew. The boys kept up their soccer games near the garbage bins where Srulik lost his mother. Each time they returned there, Srulik looked to see whether his mother was waiting for him.

Yoyneh kept his promise and went to the Jewish ghetto police, but no child had been reported missing. There was just a long list of nameless children who had died in the streets and were known only by the addresses of the houses by which they were found.

Whenever their rovings brought them to a new part of

the ghetto, Yankel asked, "Srulik, was it near here?"

Srulik would look hard at his surroundings. He never recognized them. If he had stayed with Yankel's gang long enough, he might have found his house in the end. But one day there were shouts in the streets, accompanied by the harsh whistles of the ghetto police.

"A roundup!"

This was something new. The shouts came from men and women running from the police. They wanted to warn others. The street emptied at once.

Yankel led the gang through some backyards to another street.

"Let's ask Yoyneh," he said. "Maybe he knows what it's about."

Yoyneh was mending a shoe stretched upside-down on a shoehorn.

"Everyone's shouting 'roundup,'" Yankel told him.

Yoyneh nodded sadly. "The Jewish police," he said, "are rounding up Jews for the Germans and putting them on trains. It looks like they're planning to empty the ghetto."

"Trains for where?"

"Resettlement."

"Where?"

Yoyneh pointed with a finger at the sky and moved his shoemaker's stool into his cubbyhole. "I'm closing," he said. "I have a wife and children to worry about. You boys should get out of the ghetto."

"Where to?"

"The Polish side."

16

"I was already there," Srulik said. "The Germans caught us."

"Get out," Yoyneh repeated. He locked the door, glanced at the keys in his hand, put them in his pocket, and went off.

The boys sat on the sidewalk, talking things over.

"There's a gate to the ghetto that always has wagons by it," Yankel said. "They come to haul away the garbage. Maybe we can hide in them."

He led them to the gate. They followed him somberly, stopping to survey it from afar. There were two German soldiers armed with rifles and four policemen—two Poles on the Polish side and two Jews on the Jewish side. The wagons, hitched to horses, stood inside the gate.

"The first to make it through," Yankel said, "gets out at the first corner and waits for the rest of us. If there are more than two of you, you'll have to hide."

"For how long?"

"For as long as it takes for all of us to cross. If we don't all make it, go without us."

"Where?"

"Search me."

They split up. Srulik inched toward the wagons, which stood parked in a row inside the gate. One began to move. He jumped onto the back and burrowed into the pile of garbage. The smell didn't bother him. The farmer whose wagon it was heard the sound and turned around. For a second, as Srulik disappeared, their eyes met. The farmer hesitated. Then Srulik heard the crack of his whip and the cry:

"Giddy-up!"

The wagon lurched over some cobblestones and stopped. There were Polish and German voices, and then they set out again. Then a German shouted behind them: *"Halt!"*

The wagon came to a stop. A soldier ran toward it on studded boots. He made a German remark and Srulik felt something cold slide past his right leg, rip his pants, and slice into the heap of garbage. It withdrew and plunged back two more hair-raising times, once close to his head.

"Get a move on!" the German said in Polish. "There's no boy in there."

The wagon set out again. The rattle of the wheels and the clip-clop of the horse's hooves made Srulik feel hopeful. But now came more shouts—this time far away. The wagon stopped once more. Srulik raised himself and peered out from the rear. The German soldier and a Polish policeman were running toward them, shouting and waving their hands. The farmer leaned back, yanked the frightened boy from his place, and set him down on the road. Srulik's first instinct was to run. The farmer said, "Don't move, boy. I'll get you out of here."

The policeman and the soldier were coming closer. Srulik froze. A shiver ran through him. The farmer bent over the horse with a knife and cut the harness strap. He swung Srulik onto the horse and mounted behind him, and they galloped off. Two shots rang out. Srulik tried turning around to look, but the farmer gripped him tightly. When he finally caught a glimpse over his shoulder, the gate of the ghetto had vanished, as had the soldier, the policeman, and the wagon.

After a while the horse slowed to a trot. The farmer relaxed his grip, and Srulik breathed a sigh of relief. It was the first horse he had ever ridden in his life.

They left the city behind them. Before long they were riding through fields with woods on either side. Now and then they passed a solitary cottage. After a while they came to a village of thatch-roofed houses. Each house had a vegetable garden with some fruit trees and small buildings around it. Srulik saw horses, cows, pigs, and chickens in the farmyards. Wash hung from laundry lines, and here and there an empty pot was drying upside-down on a fence post.

They rode through the village. A barking dog chased them. A woman sitting in her doorway with a child watched them go by. Boys played soccer on the road. The farmer reined the horse to a walk to keep it from kicking up dust at them. He didn't speak. Neither did Srulik. They left the village. Another village appeared on the horizon, and the farmer stopped and pointed. Srulik looked and saw several boys dressed in rags by a stream that sparkled in the sunlight. The boys noticed them and dived into the reeds along the bank.

"Those are Jewish children," the farmer said. "Go to them."

He dismounted and helped Srulik down, then took two cubes of sugar and a piece of bread from his pocket. He gave Srulik one cube and the bread and fed the other cube to the horse, patting its neck fondly. Putting his hand on Srulik's head, he made the sign of the cross over him and said, "May the Mother of God look after you."

He mounted his horse and rode off. Srulik watched him

19

go. He wanted to wave goodbye, but the farmer didn't turn around. Should he eat the bread and sugar together, or first one and then the other? He decided to eat the bread first. He chewed it as he watched the farmer grow smaller in the distance and vanish around a bend in the road. Then he ate the sugar.

3.

The Forest Protects Us

Srulik cut across the field and went to look for the boys who had hidden by the stream bank. Although from the horse he had seen the spot clearly, he now he had to guess where it was. Soon, he found it. The boys were sitting by the water, having an argument. They fell silent when they saw him. After a while one of them said, "That's the red-head we saw on the farmer's horse."

"Was that you?" a boy asked.

Srulik nodded.

"Where are you from?"

"The Warsaw ghetto," he said.

"When did you leave it?"

"Today."

"What were you doing on that horse?"

Srulik shrugged.

"You don't know?" The question was accompanied by an incredulous laugh.

"No."

"What happened to its wagon?" someone asked. "It was dragging its harness."

Srulik told them what happened and showed them his

21

ripped pants. He also, he now discovered, had a bloody cut on his foot.

"You're lucky. That German had a bayonet."

"Do you have anything to eat?" Srulik asked.

A boy took some farmer's cheese from his pocket. Srulik broke off a piece, ate it, and licked his fingers.

"Where did you get this cheese from?" he asked.

"The Poles hang it in bags from their fences to dry. It's easy to steal it," the boy said.

There was a consultation.

"What should we do with him?"

"One little brat is enough."

"Don't you even care about him, Shleymi?" asked a small boy who was sharpening a pocket knife on a stone.

"You keep out of this, Yosele," Shleymi said. "Be happy we agreed to take you."

Apart from the boy with the knife, everyone was older than Srulik.

"Let Avrum decide," the boy with the cheese declared.

Everyone looked at Avrum.

"We'll take him," he said.

"If he does something dumb that gets us caught, you're to blame," Shleymi told him.

The boy with the cheese said, "Once we're caught, who cares who's to blame?"

His name was Itsik. He sat by the stream, throwing sticks into the water and watching them float away on the current. Srulik lay on his back and gazed at the sky. He kept picturing the farmer and his horse growing smaller in the distance. His thoughts were full of the day's events.

✡

Someone was waking him.

"Come on, we're moving out."

It was little Yosele. He was barefoot and wearing a grown man's clothes with the pants hitched up to his waist and tied with a rope. Srulik saw that he was the only boy with shoes. They didn't look like they would last long, because Yoyneh had never managed to mend them.

The boys set out on a path that led through some fields toward a far-off village. When they neared it, they took cover in a wheat field. Some people and animals were visible in the nearest farmyard. The sun was setting. A mare stood tethered by a stable, its little foal scampering around it. A girl was coming home with a flock of geese. A dog barked a greeting and the geese crooked their necks at it with fearsome shrieks. A teenage boy led some cows to a barn. A woman stepped out of a house and shouted at him:

"Yacek, get those pigs into the sty!"

Wasn't that the Polish name that was supposed to appear on the postcard his parents had planned to send to his brothers and sister?

The woman, her sleeves rolled up, went to the barn. She held a milk can in one hand and a milking stool in the other. Avrum studied the farmyard.

"They've prepared baskets of vegetables to take to the market tomorrow," he whispered.

What happened next was unexpected. The farmer strode out of the house, saddled the mare, and rode off. The little foal ran after them. The dog jumped to its feet and went with them. The boys excitedly watched them go. Then Avrum said, "Now!"

They jumped from their hiding places and ran to the farmyard. The large baskets of vegetables were standing by a wall, next to a smaller basket of eggs. Avrum grabbed the eggs while the others snatched cucumbers, tomatoes, carrots, and radishes and stuffed pockets and bags of cheesecloth with them. The geese shrieked. The boys took off at a run. The teenage boy looked out from the pigsty to see what was happening and yelled, "Yids! Thieves! Mama!"

His mother stepped out of the barn.

"The eggs!" the Polish boy yelled.

They all ran as fast as they could, with Avrum and Shleymi taking the lead. The Polish boy gave chase and caught up with a straggler who had started to run a moment too late. He tackled him and pinned him to the ground. The boy screamed and cried. The woman went on chasing the rest of them, falling farther and farther behind until she gave up.

They stopped to catch their breath, grinning as they inspected the vegetables. Their mouths watered when they saw the eggs in Avrum's basket. No one mentioned the boy who was caught.

"In the city we only stole when it was dark," Srulik said.

"You can't steal in the dark from the fields," Itsik explained. "You have to see what you're picking."

"And if you're looking for something to wear," Yosele added, "you have to see what's hanging on the clothesline."

Now Srulik understood where Yosele's clothes came from.

"This isn't the city," said Shleymi. "Everything is

24

different here. You have to be careful not to do anything dumb."

"Like what?" Srulik asked.

"Like talking to Poles. Or swimming naked in the river. You mustn't ever take off your pants."

Srulik had never heard of such a rule. But although he couldn't think of the reason for it, he didn't want to ask Shleymi.

They passed a farm. Some pear trees stood in front of the farmhouse. "They're real pears," Itsik said of the fruit. "Not like the little sour ones you sometimes see by the road."

They crept up stealthily. There was no barking.

"There's no dog."

"Let Srulik pick some pears," Shleymi said.

"Why Srulik?" Avrum asked.

"Why not? It's time he did something."

"Can you climb a tree?" Avrum asked.

"Of course."

Itsik gave Srulik a small bag. The boys watched him tensely. In Blonie, Srulik had climbed trees all the time. He scrambled up a fence and shinnied into a tree. But the dog had only been asleep. Now it woke behind the house and began to bark. An old farmer stepped outside and saw Srulik in the tree. Srulik jumped back over the fence and ran. The farmer freed the dog and they ran after him.

"Stop, thief!" the farmer shouted.

The boys lit out before Srulik reached them. Although he could easily outrun the farmer, the dog was catching up. He stopped short, took a pear from the bag, and flung it at it as hard as he could. It hit its target and the dog howled and stopped, too. But it didn't stop barking, and Srulik didn't know what to do. If he started to run again, so would the dog, and if he didn't, the farmer would soon be there. Avrum, seeing his predicament, turned back to lend a hand. Shleymi grabbed him.

"Don't! The farmer will catch you both."

"Let go of me," Avrum growled and broke loose.

He ran back and hit the dog with a stick. The dog lunged at him. But Avrum had been in fights with village dogs before. He whacked it on the snout and it ran off with its tail between its legs before the farmer could reach them.

Srulik couldn't stop thinking about the boy who had been caught.

✡

The boys came to a broad meadow and walked through the grass. Cows and horses were grazing in it. Three other boys were sitting by a fire. Avrum halted. He gave Yosele two small coins and said, "Go ask if they'll sell us some matches."

Srulik went with him.

"Do you have any matches?" they asked.

The Polish boys shook their heads.

"We'll pay you for them," Yosele said.

"Then I reckon we've got some," said a boy.

Yosele examined the box of matches he was given. It wasn't full. The boy filled it from a second box, and Yosele handed him the coins. Colored bottles were lying by the fire. Some were broken, and others were neatly sliced in half.

"Are you making glasses from those bottles?" Srulik asked.

"What's it to you?"

Yosele leaned down and took two broken bits of bottle.

"You have to pay for that too."

"Try to make me," Yosele said.

The Polish boys said nothing. From time to time they cast suspicious glances at the bigger boys standing on the path.

"Let's go," Yosele said.

He gave the matches to Avrum and they continued on their way. Yosele and Srulik brought up the rear.

"How come Avrum sent us to buy the matches?" Srulik wanted to know.

"We're too small to scare the Polish kids."

"But why did you take those broken bottles?"

"They're for you." Yosele handed him the two pieces of glass.

Srulik didn't get it.

"They're in place of a knife."

"Who else has one?"

"Just me."

"Where did you get it?"

"I found it in the forest."

Srulik examined the broken glass.

"You have it to wrap it rags so it won't cut you."

"I don't have any rags," Srulik said.

"Cut some from your shirt."

Srulik took a piece of jagged glass and cut off part of his shirt sleeve.

The sun had set. The black line of the forest in the distance was now a row of trees. They sat down to eat in the fading light instead of waiting to reach the forest. Srulik had never eaten a raw egg before. Yosele showed him how to make two small holes at either end with a toothpick and to suck it out through one.

"Why don't you use your knife?" Srulik asked.

"The blade's broken. Look." Yosele opened the knife.

No one mentioned the boy who had been caught. "What will happen to him?" Srulik wanted to know.

"He'll be beaten and handed over to the Germans for money or vodka," Itsik said.

"And then?"

"No one who was caught has ever come back to tell us."

"Don't talk so much," Shleymi scolded them.

They went on eating in silence. When they were done, they put the leftover vegetables in their pockets and bags and set out again. It was dark, but the darkness was different from the ghetto's. The land loomed around them, as flat as the palm of a hand, and the vast sky overhead was strewn with stars. Just as they entered the forest, a big orange moon came up. Srulik remembered moons like that from Blonie. In the ghetto, he had never seen one. They were almost in the forest now. "Where are we going?" Srulik asked.

"Into the forest to sleep."

He was scared. He had gone to the forest with his older brothers during the day to gather mushrooms and pick blueberries, but at night it was a scary place. They passed the tree line and kept walking.

"Hold hands," Avrum said.

Srulik gave one hand to Yosele and the other to Itsik. They came to a place where they stopped and lay down. For a few minutes there was low conversation. Srulik lay with his eyes shut. Then he opened them wide. The forest was talking. He listened. Was it the same forest as the big one near Blonie? The moon was hidden behind the treetops. Here and there a patch of sky shone brightly through the darkness. Stars glittered. The silhouettes of the branches were outlined against the sky. Srulik heard a strange sound, like someone groaning or breathing. He gave a start.

"What's that?" he whispered.

Yosele, lying beside him, whispered back, "An owl."

"Aren't you afraid to be here at night?"

"Don't you see, Srulik?" Yosele said. "If not for the forest, the farmers would have caught us long ago. It's this darkness that keeps them from finding us and handing us over to the Germans the way they'll hand over Leybele. It protects us. That's why I like it. The darkness keeps us alive. Do you see now?"

"Yes."

"Are you still afraid?"

"Yes," Srulik admitted.

"You'll get used to it. I was afraid too."

"How did you meet the other boys?"

"I heard them talking. Their Polish sounded Jewish, so I went to them. At first Shleymi didn't want to take me."

Srulik suddenly realized why Shleymi had told him not to talk to Poles. "Do I talk Polish like a Jew too?" he asked.

"No. Neither does Avrum. But some of us have Yiddish accents. Like Shleymi."

"And why shouldn't I go swimming or take my pants off?"

"Because you're circumcised."

"Aren't the Poles?"

Yosele laughed. "No. Only the Jews."

Yosele was from Warsaw. His mother, he told Srulik, made a living in the ghetto by sewing and selling the blue stars of David that Jews had to wear on their sleeves. With the money she made, he had bought potatoes and bread on the Polish side of the wall and smuggled them to the Jewish side. It was hard, dangerous work. Twice he had been caught. Each time he was beaten and the food was taken from him. Before being taken to the hospital with typhus, his mother said to him, "Yosele, cross to the Polish side and don't come back."

"And you've been in the forest ever since then?" Srulik asked.

"No. At first I hung around the villages. Until I was almost caught."

"Couldn't we be caught in the forest, too?"

"No one goes very deep into it. Except for the partisans."

"Who are they?"

"Poles who fight the Germans. They don't want any part of us, though. You have to watch out for the forester, too. He turns Jews in."

"Are all the Poles bad?"

Yosele thought. "No. Once I knocked on a door and they gave me food without any questions."

"Are we deep in the forest now?"

"Not yet. In the dark it's safe here too. In the morning we'll go deeper."

The next morning, Yosele awoke him. Srulik was surprised to open his eyes and see trees and branches instead of walls and a ceiling. Then he remembered where he was. He was hungry and thirsty.

"Come," Yosele said. "We're going to our hideout."

Avrum led them through the trees to a brook. They stopped to drink, scooping water with their hands or lapping it while lying on their stomachs. Srulik stuck his head in the water. It felt good flowing over him. He opened his mouth and drank.

They took out their vegetables. Avrum put the basket of eggs in the middle. When they finished eating, they stored everything in a hollow tree trunk and went to look for berries—wild strawberries, raspberries, blueberries, and red and black currants. They also picked white and black mulberries from the trees and little green nuts whose shells were still soft.

Srulik found some mushrooms. They were the kind he had gathered with his brother in the forest near Blonie. His new friends were afraid to eat them.

"Srulik," Avrum said, "you'll die from them."

He ate them anyway, and his friends learned.

Late that afternoon, Avrum led them back to their hideout. They drank from the brook and ate more vegetables and eggs.

"How can Avrum always find the way?" Srulik asked.

"Partly by the moss and partly . . . I don't really know," Itsik said.

31

"What's moss?"

Itsik showed him some growing on the tree trunks. "You see," he said, "it only grows on one side of the tree. And no matter how many trees you look at, it's always the same side. It helps you to find your way back."

Srulik didn't understand.

"How?"

"By following it in the opposite direction."

Although this made no sense to him either, he didn't ask again. He would try to figure it out for himself.

"Do you have any more farmer's cheese?" he asked.

Itsik laughed. "No. We finished that long ago. We'll steal some more when we can."

The next night Srulik slept near Yosele again. They talked quietly before falling asleep.

"You know something?" Yosele whispered. "Trees have souls."

"Who told you?"

"Leybele. He said their souls go places at night."

"Was he your friend?"

"Yes."

"Are the souls of trees good or bad?"

"They must be good. No tree ever harmed anyone."

Srulik thought about that. "Do you think it hurts a tree to break its branches?" he asked.

"Maybe no more than clipping your fingernails," said Yosele.

"My mother always threw the clippings from my fingernails into the oven," Srulik told him. "First she mixed them with feathers."

"So did mine. Without the feathers. You know why?"

"Why?"

"So that your soul won't look for them on Judgment Day."

"What's Judgment Day?"

"The end of the world. When all the dead rise."

"Everyone?"

"That's what my grandpa says. I'll see my mother again. And she won't be sick anymore."

Srulik sighed. "I wish I knew what happened to my mother."

"What about your father?"

He told Yosele of the time they tried escaping the ghetto and the German soldiers appeared on motorcycles.

"I can't remember my father," Yosele said. "He died when I was little. We lived with my grandfather. He was a bookseller."

"Can you read?"

"Yes. Can you?"

"No."

When he was little, Srulik had gone to Hebrew school. All they had learned there were the Hebrew letters. The Polish letters were different.

"What did your father do?" Yosele asked.

"He was a baker. Sometimes he took me to his bakery to sleep on top of the oven. In the morning he woke me and gave me the first hot rolls to eat."

Srulik's mouth watered, thinking of those rolls.

"Do you have brothers?" he asked Yosele.

"No."

"I have two. And two sisters."

"Where are they?"

"I don't know. Maybe they're dead. They were probably caught in some roundup."

"What's a roundup?" Yosele asked.

"That's when the Jewish police and the German soldiers take the Jews to trains for resettlement."

"Where?"

"In the sky," Srulik said.

"Who told you?"

"Yoyneh the shoemaker."

Yosele thought about that. "I'm glad my mother's dead," he said at last.

4.

Baked Birds

The next day Avrum and Itsik went to hunt birds with a slingshot. They returned at noon with a slew of birds, tied by the feet and slung over their shoulders. The biggest of them was the size of a chicken. Avrum said it was called a woodcock. Srulik was disappointed to be told that he would have to wait until evening for the birds to be cooked and eaten.

"Why?" he asked.

"Because the smoke from the fire could be seen."

When it grew dark, they built a low wall of branches around the site of the fire to keep the flames from being seen. Shleymi and Avrum cleaned the birds, cutting off their heads, with Yosele's pocketknife and a piece of jagged glass. Mud was brought from the stream bank and each bird was coated with it. When the fire had burned down to hot coals, the mud-coated birds were put in it to bake while they all waited.

"Give me my knife," Yosele said to Shleymi.

Shleymi stuck it in his pocket. "It's mine now," he said.

"Let him have it," Srulik said.

Shleymi gave Srulik a push. The boys all jumped to their

feet. Avrum took command, and Shleymi returned the knife grudgingly.

They took the smaller mud-birds from the fire first. The bigger ones had to bake a while longer. The mud had hardened and turned to clay. They rolled it on the ground to cool it and then cracked it with stones and peeled it off. The feathers came with it, leaving the birds ready to eat.

When they went to sleep that night, Srulik and Yosele lay down side by side as usual. Srulik was still mad at being pushed by Shleymi.

"Shleymi was king around here until Avrum came along," Yosele told him.

"Is Avrum stronger?"

"I don't know. But he never gets lost in the forest."

"Boy, that was good," Srulik said, licking his lips. "When will they hunt some more?"

"Not for a while."

"Why not?"

"Avrum's afraid the fire will give us away."

Srulik sighed with disappointment. "Too bad," he said.

"You know," Yosele told him, "in the beginning, when I was all by myself, I was so hungry that I ate everything. I even ate snails. They're disgusting, but I didn't bite into them. I just swallowed them as fast as I could."

"I could never do that," Srulik said disgustedly.

"When you're hungry enough, you can do anything. Once I found a rabbit in a trap. I didn't have this knife, so I cut it up with a piece of glass. And I didn't have any matches, so I ate it raw."

"You didn't die from it?"

"You can see I didn't."

In the morning Srulik awoke with a start. What he had heard wasn't a dream. It was real. There were shots, coming from nearby and echoing all around him. Then there were shouts and orders being given in German.

He jumped up and ran as fast as he could in the opposite direction. After a while, when there was no longer anything around him but silence, he stopped.

He didn't know where he was. He tried remembering what he had been told about moss growing only on one side of trees, but he had no idea how this might help him to find the other boys. All he could think of doing was to shout.

"Yosele! Avrum!"

His own voice echoing through the forest scared him. Someone was coming. Srulik hid. It was Shleymi. He jumped from his hiding place, happy to see him.

"Shout like that again and we'll be caught for sure," Shleymi said. "I knew you couldn't be trusted."

"Where is everyone?" Srulik asked worriedly.

"Instead of hiding, they all ran off like dopes."

"You also ran off like a dope," Srulik said.

"You'd better watch it," Shleymi threatened. "There's no one here but the two of us."

Srulik said nothing. After a while he asked, "Where do we go now?"

"I want to find the stream," Shleymi said.

"Can you?"

"That's enough out of you."

Suddenly, Shleymi stopped in his tracks. Someone was lying between two trees. It was a grown man. They tensed, ready to turn and run. But the man didn't move.

His head lay in a puddle of congealed blood.

"He's dead," Srulik whispered.

The dead man's arm extended forward. Something lay by its hand. Shleymi bent to look at it. It was a pair of glasses. He knelt by the man's side.

"Let's go," Srulik said.

"You go," said Shleymi.

Srulik walked away. Feeling sick, he sat on the ground and watched as Shleymi went through the dead man's pants pockets and pulled papers and objects out of them. Then he turned the man on his back and stuck his hand in the man's jacket pocket. Finished, he straightened up. "Srulik?" he called softly.

He doesn't see me, Srulik thought. He didn't answer or budge. Shleymi called again. When there was no response, he began to look for Srulik, carefully poking at the undergrowth. But he was walking the wrong way. Something in Srulik wanted to run after him. He opened his mouth to speak. But nothing came out. It was better to be alone than with Shleymi.

Toward evening the sky clouded over and cast its pall over the forest.

Srulik decided to sleep in a tree. He climbed a big oak and found a comfortable spot in the cleft of two big branches. Yet he couldn't fall asleep. Would he find the other boys? And how would he manage in the forest if he didn't? He reached for his butterfly pin. But the butterfly had spent too much time in his pocket and hardly glowed.

In the morning he decided to look for Poles—the good ones that gave you food when you knocked on their door. He walked for a long time. He was thirsty. When he came to a puddle of rainwater, he bent down to drink. Little bugs were crawling in it. He shut his eyes and drank anyway.

Suddenly he found himself in a familiar place. He looked around him. There was the tree with the hollow trunk! He felt as happy as if he had come home from a long journey. He ran to drink from the brook and poked through the ashes of the fire until he found a little bird cased in mud. There were still some vegetables and eggs in the tree trunk. He decided to stay put and wait.

He slept in the tree that night, too. The next morning he performed an experiment, walking carefully away from the brook while watching the moss on the trees. Then he stopped and walked back the other way. Now he understood how to tell directions from the moss. He left the brook again, stopping to look back now and then. From time to time he halted to pick berries. A snail was crawling on a bush, its two horns groping in front of it. No, that was one thing he never would eat. He reached a blackberry bush, turned around, and managed to find his way back. He wished Yosele were there to tell about it.

Slipping down from his tree to the ground on the morning of the third day, Srulik knew he had lost the boys for good. He drank from the brook, ate the last two eggs in the tree trunk, and walked off without turning back. His eyes strained to make out a patch of clear light that would tell him where the forest ended. But he saw none and in the end he grew tired and sat helplessly on the ground.

Someone was coming. He crawled into a bush to hide. From it he saw a man in an official-looking cap and green jacket walking toward him with a rifle on his shoulder. It must be the forester who turns Jews over to the Germans, he thought. Perhaps the man was on his way home. Did foresters live in forests or villages? Srulik decided to follow him. The forester walked along a narrow path for a long while. Eventually Srulik spied some light between the trees. He waited until the forester was gone and stepped back out into the world.

The path grew wider, winding through fields until it reached a village. Srulik knocked on the door of the first house he came to. A woman opened it. He looked at her without a word. She looked at him. "Come on in," she said after a while.

She asked no questions, just as Yosele had said. It was as if she knew exactly who he was. She sat him at a table and gave him a big slice of bread and a glass of milk. He wolfed it all down. He couldn't remember when he had last seen fresh bread and milk. A small child was playing in the corner with some pieces of wood. The woman sat beside the child with some food. She called him "Jurek" and fed him with a spoon.

"Who's there?" a man's voice asked.

"A boy," said the woman.

Her husband entered the room and regarded Srulik thoughtfully.

"Would you like to stay and work on the farm?" he asked after a long silence.

"Yes," Srulik said.

"Finish eating and I'll give you something to do."

Srulik finished eating. The farmer returned, wearing his coat and boots. He led Srulik outside and took him to a storeroom full of differently sized and colored bottles.

"Arrange all the bottles on the shelves by size and color," he said. "Do a good job."

Srulik nodded.

The farmer left. "I'm shutting the door so that no one bothers you," he said.

Srulik set to work. Suddenly he heard a key turn in the lock. Alarmed, he went to the door and put his eye to a crack between its wooden planks. At first he saw nothing. Then he spied the farmer pushing a motorcycle. The man mounted it, started it up, and drove off. Srulik tried opening the door. It was locked. He tried breaking it but couldn't. Panicky, he ran around the room like an animal caught in a trap, screaming and knocking bottles off their shelves.

"Just a minute, I'll let you out!" It was the woman, standing outside.

Srulik calmed down. He heard banging noises. The woman smashed the lock with an ax and opened the door.

"Run, boy!" she said. "Run!"

5.

Alone in the Forest

Srulik returned to the forest. It seemed happy to have him back. Although it was the same forest he had left that morning, it was also a different one. It was his and Yosele's forest that protected and saved them. For the first time, Srulik felt love for it. He walked deeper and deeper into it until he came to a dark, entangled hiding place.

In the following weeks, he slept in trees and learned to climb them like a monkey. He clambered up them and leaped from tree to tree by swinging on the branches. His shoes had fallen apart long ago. The soles of his feet grew so tough that he could run on anything without feeling pain. He learned to move as stealthily as the forest animals and to treat infected scratches from bushes and vines by lancing them with a pine needle, squeezing out the pus, and disinfecting them with his own urine.

In daytime, he rarely thought of his friends or felt lonely. He was too busy looking for food and water and observing everything around him. He was fascinated by every animal and bird, by every sound that he heard and movement that he saw.

Yet at night, when he crawled into a tree, all kinds of thoughts ran through his mind. Of Yosele. Of Yankel. Of his mother. Even of Yoyneh the shoemaker. Sometimes he woke in a fright, startled by the cry of an animal or night bird.

He stopped counting the days. He lived from minute to minute, hour to hour, morning to evening. He drank rainwater from puddles and ate berries. While roaming in the forest one day, he came to a brook like the one his gang of boys had camped by. From then on he returned to it every evening, guiding himself by the moss on the trees.

He didn't have a slingshot, but he did have a good throwing arm. He took some smooth stones from the bottom of the brook, whittled a thick stick with his piece of glass, found a small clearing in the forest, and sat waiting in perfect stillness against the trunk of a tree. At first little animals appeared, darting in and out of sight. Although he didn't believe he could hit any of them with a stone, it was fun to watch them. Sometimes a chipmunk stopped to look at him anxiously, sniffing at him from a distance before it disappeared. After a while a doe came along with her fawn. He sat motionless while she stared at him, trying to guess what sort of creature he was. Then, with a single bound so quick it was almost invisible, they were gone. He went on sitting there. The noise of something large shuffling through the undergrowth told him wild boar were approaching. Soon a couple appeared with its piglets. They looked like the village pigs but were furry and had long, scary tusks. Srulik scrambled into a tree without waiting to see if they noticed him.

He had climbed down and returned to his place when a hedgehog entered the clearing. Srulik fell upon it with his stick. The hedgehog rolled itself into a ball, its quills bristling. Srulik thrust his stick against the round form and pressed with all his might until it ceased to stir. Then he turned it over and slit its belly with his piece of glass. At night he lit a fire and singed the hedgehog over it. This made it easier to cut away the skin and quills. He carved chunks of meat and roasted them on a spit.

A few days went by before he succeeded again. This time he killed a squirrel with a stone. He cut off its head, skinned and cleaned it, and rinsed it in the brook. Then, too hungry to wait, he ate it raw. He was no longer sure he wouldn't eat snails like Yosele.

✡

"What are you doing here, boy?"

Srulik gave a start. He hadn't heard a human voice in a long while. It was the forester. Srulik recognized him. He just didn't recognize Srulik.

"Picking berries," Srulik said.

"I can see that."

The man regarded him. He was barefoot like a farm boy and dressed in rags like a homeless orphan.

"Where are your parents?"

"I don't have any."

"Where are you from?"

Srulik shrugged.

"Are you a Jew?"

"No."

"What's your name?"

"Jurek."

"What's your family's name?"

"I don't know."

The man took a minute to digest this. Then he said,

"My sister is looking for a boy to take the cows and sheep to pasture."

Srulik didn't know what to say. He remembered being locked in the bottle room. But he missed human contact. The man smiled at him. It looked like a smile he could trust. It was hard to believe he was someone who turned Jewish boys in to the Germans.

"Look, son. When autumn comes, you'll die of hunger and cold. My sister's farm is outside the village. You'll be safe there."

Srulik wanted to say that he was safe here too, but he didn't. He could tell the man knew he was Jewish. And yet he was asking him nicely. He could just as well have taken him prisoner by surprise.

"My sister lives near the forest. You can always come back here," the forester added.

"All right," Srulik agreed.

He followed the forester. Although a patch of light shining through the trees made him think they were nearly out of the forest, it turned out to come from a large clearing in which the forester's house stood. A dog came to greet them, wagging its tail. Behind it came a woman with a baby.

"Who do you have there?" she asked.

"A boy to work for my sister."

"Like the one who worked for us?"

"Something like that."

"Come, boy," the woman said. "I'll give you something to eat."

She left him alone with a bowl of potatoes mashed with lard and fried onions. He gobbled it up. A half-eaten loaf of bread was on the table. Though he didn't know if it was meant for him, Srulik kept eating chunks from it even after he was bursting. When he couldn't stuff himself any more, he cut a last piece of bread and hid it in his pocket. Meanwhile, the forester led a horse from the stable, saddled it, and sat Srulik on the saddle in front of him.

They rode as far as a small farmhouse next to a field of potatoes. The village beyond it was indeed close to the forest. Two barking dogs ran toward them, then calmed down and wagged their tails. A woman stepped out of the house. The forester dismounted and gave her a hug. Whispering something to her, he lowered Srulik from the horse. The dogs sniffed at him. He was frightened.

"Don't be scared," the woman said. "They're friendly dogs."

A few auxiliary buildings stood around the farmhouse. There was a barn, a sheep shed, and a storeroom. In front of the house were some fruit trees and rows of vegetables. Chickens ran in the yard. A sow lay on the ground, nursing her litter.

"Wait for me here," the woman said, stepping into the house with her brother. Srulik stayed in the yard with the dogs. He took the bread from his pocket and chewed it slowly. The dogs approached him to see what he was eating. He rolled a ball of dough between his fingers and offered it to one of them. The dog lunged for it. Scared, he dropped it and the dog caught it in midair. Then the second dog came for his share. This time Srulik held on to the dough until the dog took it from him gently. He went on eating while feeding the dogs between one bite and the next. They're friendly, he thought, repeating the woman's words. He reached out to pet one. The other came to be petted, too.

The forester and his sister emerged from the house. The man slung his rifle on his shoulder, mounted the horse, and nodded to Srulik. "Be a good boy," he told him.

His sister waved. Then she told Srulik to come to the barn. The dogs followed them. Inside were three cows and two small calves lying in some straw. The woman showed Srulik how to fill their feed stalls with hay and how to lock the barn door when he left.

"Now repeat what I told you," she said.

He passed the test with flying colors.

She took a bucket and sat down to milk the cows. Srulik watched.

"Bring me that cup hanging on the wall," she said, pointing with her chin.

He took a tin cup from its rusty nail and brought it to her. She filled it with milk and handed it back.

"Drink, son. What's your name?"

"Jurek," Srulik said.

He gulped the warm milk eagerly. When he had finished, the woman told him to rinse the cup beneath a spigot and hang it on its nail.

"Why don't you milk her, too?" he asked, pointing to the third cow.

"Don't you see how fat she is? She's about to give birth. When she does, she'll have milk."

Next she brought him to the sheep shed. The four sheep bleated when they saw her. She showed Srulik how to feed them, took him to the well, and showed him how to draw water. The well was round and deep with a white brick enclosure and a little roof that rested on two columns. Beneath the roof was a log with a rope, attached to a crank. The other end of the rope dangled into the well. The woman leaned over the well and called down into it. Her voice echoed back. Srulik stood on tiptoe to clear the brick wall and called, "Aho-o-o-o-oyyy!"

His call echoed too. The woman smiled at him and he smiled back. She showed him how to draw water by turning the log with the crank, but the crank was too high for him to reach. He looked around the yard, saw an empty crate, brought it to stand on, and cranked up a bucket of water. The woman praised him for using his head. She took the bucket and filled the cows' drinking trough. It took three buckets to be full. Then she showed Srulik how to fill the sheep's trough.

"All right," she said. "Now go to sleep. In the morning I'll teach you to take the cows and the sheep to pasture."

He looked around the shed. "Sleep where?"

"Make yourself a bed with some straw."

She called the dogs and left Srulik with the sheep. Sleeping on straw was fine with him. At home, his mother had stuffed their mattresses with it.

In the middle of the night he was woken by the sound of rain. A cold wind blew through the open window of the shed. Too drowsy to think, he crawled in among the sheep and fell back asleep.

When the woman came to wake him in the morning, it was a beautiful, sunny day. The only sign of the rain were the puddles in the yard. He followed her to the barn. She milked the cows and gave him a cup of milk to drink again. Then she slung a knapsack over his shoulder, handed him a walking stick, showed him how to drive the cows and sheep ahead of him, and accompanied him to the pasture. The two dogs came, too. It wasn't far from the farm to a broad, green meadow.

"Your job is to keep the cows and sheep from wandering into the neighbor's field," she explained. "That's all you have to do. When the sun is low, bring them home."

"How?"

"Just say: 'Home, girls!' You'll see they know the way better than you do."

She pointed to the knapsack and said, "There's a lunch for you there. Eat it at noontime."

"How will I know when it's noontime?"

The woman laughed.

"That's when the sun is directly overhead. You'll learn. In the evening, you'll eat your supper with me."

She called to the dogs. "Once you're friends with them," she said, "you can take them along with you."

Srulik didn't wait for the sun to be overhead before examining the knapsack. There was half a loaf of bread, a bottle of water, and some farmer's cheese wrapped in newspaper. He ate some bread and cheese and left the rest for later.

The work was easy. Although he was more frightened of the cows than of the sheep, he was able to head them off each time they neared the neighbor's field by shouting and waving his stick. To his surprise, they obeyed him. Instead of using their horns to drive him off and go where they wanted, they backed away and returned to the meadow.

The day passed without a dull moment. He lay in the grass and watched the cows eat, cropping the grass with their tongues. Strangely, they had no upper teeth. The sheep, on the other hand, used their lips and teeth as though they were eating from a plate. When he was tired of studying them, he turned his attention to the grass in front of him. Beetles, ants, and other little bugs were crawling around in it. It was a different world from in the rotting leaves and pine needles on the damp forest floor. A brightly colored butterfly flew by and he raised himself on his elbows to follow its flight. He didn't want to risk hurting it by trying to catch it. He did try catching some darning needles—without success.

Two boys were pasturing cows in the distance. He gazed at them, wondering if they might someday become friends. One was in charge of some cows and the other of a few sheep. In a meadow nearer to him was a girl. She was guarding two cows who were tethered to a stake in the ground.

The sun began to set. Big and red, it sank into the clouds on the horizon. Srulik brandished his stick and called out: "Home, girls!"

To his astonishment, the cows lifted their heads, mooed in agreement, and began walking back to the farmhouse. The sheep followed.

They entered the farmyard. The dogs let out a few barks and ran to greet them, tails wagging. The woman fed the cows and sent Srulik to water and feed the sheep. By the time he returned to the barn, she was done milking. She told him to wash at the trough and join her in the house.

The house had only one room, just like their old house in Blonie. The stove was lit and food was cooking, filling the room with a mouth-watering smell. The woman sat him at a table and filled two plates. On them was an omelet and noodles mixed with something orange.

"It's pumpkin," said the woman. "Don't you know what that is?"

"No," Srulik said.

"I'll show you in the garden."

She poured cream over it all and handed him a glass of milk.

"After supper, you'll take off your clothes," she said. "I'll wash them and give you something to wear while they're drying."

Later she gave him a grown man's nightshirt. Srulik took his butterfly and piece of glass from his pants pockets, undressed, and put it on.

In the morning the woman told him, "I burned all your clothes. They were so full of lice that they would have walked away by themselves if I had put them on the floor."

She gave him a large shirt with sleeves she had cut and a pair of pants she had shortened. The waist was folded over and had a rope belt.

Now I look like Yosele, Srulik thought.

He wore his new clothes to the pasture. After a while he decided to introduce himself to the two boys. Yet as soon as he started in their direction, the cows headed for the neighbor's wheat field, forcing him to turn around and hurry back. The girl was in her meadow again, too. She had the same two cows tethered to the same stake, around which they grazed in a circle. But although she was nearer and easier to reach than the boys, she was only a girl.

6.

In the Potato Field

Slowly, Srulik learned to herd the animals. He began to understand the language of the sheep and the cows and to know what they were saying and what they wanted, what it meant when they suddenly shook their heads, and who was the lead ewe. Sometimes, when he was tired and the sun wasn't setting fast enough, he took her by the ear and led her home with the three other sheep trotting after her. The cows took one look and came too. As long as he didn't overdo it, the woman didn't mind. Once, though, he came home so early that she lost her temper and locked him out of the house. She brought him his supper to the sheep shed, a bowl of plain potatoes. He didn't do it again.

Sometimes he woke in the morning before she came to rouse him. Maybe it was the rooster that woke him, or else the sheep or the dogs, who came to play with him at dawn. Once, going to draw water from the well to wash with, he saw a man slip out of the house and run off into the forest.

He didn't ask who it was.

He kept looking at the girl with the two cows. Sometimes he caught her looking at him, too. Yet she never answered when he called to her. In the end, it was the dogs who introduced them. Srulik now took them regularly to the pasture, where he played with them and sometimes wrestled and romped with them in the grass. He could feel the girl watching these games with interest.

One day she seemed to be very busy. She kept changing places and lying down in the grass as though looking at something. Srulik wondered what she was up to. At noontime he saw her light a fire. Then she sat down to eat. She must have roasted potatoes in the coals, Srulik thought. Sniffing the air, the dogs ran to her. He called to them before they reached her and they ran back. But she called too and they turned around again. It became a game between her and Srulik. After a while, she called to him:

"Hey, Red, what do you have to eat?"

"Bread and cheese!" Srulik called back.

"I've got something better!"

"What?"

"Baked birds."

"Did you give some to the dogs?"

"Just the bones."

"Will you give me some?"

"Come on over."

But although he would have liked to, the cows headed for the neighbor's field the minute he left them. They were smarter than the sheep, who paid no attention and went on eating.

"I can't," he shouted. "The cows will get into the wheat."

The girl saw his predicament and came to him. With her she brought a few baked songbirds.

"How did you catch them?" he asked.

"Don't you know?"

"No."

"Would you like me to show you?"

"Yes."

"What will you give me?"

Srulik thought.

"I don't have anything," he said.

"What's your name?"

"Jurek."

"Mine is Marisza. Are you related to Pani Nowek?"

"No."

"Then why are you staying with her?"

"Her brother found me in the forest."

"What were you doing in the forest?"

"I was living there."

"Where are your father and mother?"

"They're dead," he said, feeling his heart twinge.

Were they? Was it all right to say that? Could it make them die if they hadn't yet? And what about his brothers and sisters? The thought of them made him sad. Marisza noticed.

"I know what it's like," she said. "My parents are dead, too. That's why I was sent to my aunt and uncle in the village. They send their children to school in town and I have to watch the cows. And at night they make me serve supper and wash the dishes, and their daughter sticks out her tongue at me. They don't even take me to church on Sunday. I have to pasture the cows then, too. Do you go to church?"

"No."

"Everyone except me has a bed to sleep in," Marisza went on.

"Where do you sleep?" Srulik asked.

"In the barn."

"I sleep in the sheep shed. When it's cold, I cuddle up with the sheep."

"My aunt and uncle don't have sheep. Just cows, pigs, and chickens. Come on, I'll teach you how to catch little birds and cook them."

"I know how to cook them," Srulik said. "I had a friend in the forest who hunted them with a slingshot."

"What happened to him?"

Srulik shrugged. "He's gone."

Marisza undid her braids and plucked two long hairs from them. Laying them on the ground, she tied a small loop at the end of them. Then she made a slipknot by passing them through the loop.

"See? You put a hair in the grass and tie the other end to a stem. Then you scatter crumbs. The birds are so dumb that they step into the loop. It tightens when they try to get away. You don't believe me? When we were little my big brother caught lots of birds like that—starlings, larks, finches, sparrows, birds I can't even name."

"With hair from your braid?"

She laughed.

"I didn't have a braid then, stupid. How old are you?"

"I guess nine."

"I'm twelve," Marisza said proudly. "My brother used hair from the tail of our horse."

"Where's your brother now?"

"With my parents in Heaven. Now look and I'll show

you. You know why I'm nice to you? Because you're an orphan like me."

Srulik walked beside her. The dogs followed them. She laid the hairs in the grass, looped one end, tied the other to a stem, and scattered crumbs.

"That's all there is to it," she said. "You can go back to your cows."

Before long little birds came along to peck at the crumbs. One couldn't fly away. Marisza ran to it with Srulik on her heels. By the time he reached her, she was holding the bird in her hand. She opened the slipknot, freed it, and pocketed both hairs. "Get it?" she asked.

Srulik got it. But where was he to get such long hairs? His farm had no horse.

"Can you lend me a few hairs?" he asked.

"Sure. But we can hunt together."

They spent half the next day hunting birds. After they had caught enough of them, Marisza gathered wood and kindling for a fire. Srulik was surprised to see she had no matches.

"I'll give you some," he said.

"I have some," she told him. "But I'm going to show you a trick."

She took a round piece of glass and beamed a ray of light with it on a dry leaf. Soon there was smoke. Then a little flame appeared. Marisza added some dry pine needles and the flame flared up.

"How did you do that?" Srulik marveled.

"It's the magnifying glass that does it, not me."

"Let me try."

"First let's cook the birds."

She gave him a knife and he cut the birds' heads off and cleaned them. Marisza coated them with mud. Then she laid them in the coals and they sat down to wait.

"Once I was with my brother in the forest and we found a knapsack," she told Srulik. "There were books in it and three pieces of glass like this. The books had pictures of butterflies and bugs. They must have belonged to a nature teacher. We didn't know what the glass was for. My father taught us things you can do with it. Making a fire is just one."

Marisza showed Srulik how the glass made everything bigger: his fingertips, the grass, even a small ant.

"Let me have it for a second."

It was a wonder to him. He tried lighting a dry leaf like Marisza but couldn't do it.

"Not like that. You have to focus the light in a little point."

"What will you swap for it?"

"What do you have?"

He took out his butterfly pin. Marisza examined it and pinned it on her dress. She handed it back.

"Nope."

"But I didn't tell you yet. It shines in the dark. If you put it in the sun during the day, it gives back the sunlight during the night."

"I'll take it home with me and see. If you're right, I'll swap."

They took the cooked birds from the fire, rolled them in the grass, broke the clay, removed the little morsels, and sat down to eat. Srulik took out his water bottle. Marisza drank without touching it with her lips. When it was his turn, she said, "That's no way to drink. If you're sharing with someone, you don't let your lips touch. Don't you know that?"

He didn't. She showed him how to do it. The meat and bread were a royal feast.

"It's a lot of work," Marisza said. "But we don't have anything better to do and I love baked birds."

"Me too," said Srulik.

"I wish I could hunt grouse like the boys," Marisza said.

"How do they hunt them?"

"With slingshots."

"Are they bigger?"

"Sure. They're even bigger than a pigeon. I'll show you in the morning."

"Can't you catch them with a hair?"

"No. Not even with a horsehair. They're too strong."

The next day she gave him the magnifying glass. "Your butterfly really shines at night," she said.

She also brought him a big piece of sausage. "I stole it," she told him. "I'll split it with you if you'll play a game with me."

Srulik agreed. "What's the game?"

"Let's eat first."

After they ate, Marisza led him to the footpath that ran between the meadow and the wheat field. They sat on the hard earth and she taught him to play jacks with stones. She was awfully good at it.

"It's a girls' game," she said. "But what do you care?"

Srulik tried flipping the stones in the air and catching them like Marisza. It was hard.

"It takes time," she said. "If we play every day, you'll get better."

A sudden breeze billowed her dress.

"You're peeking!" she said. "That's dirty."

"No, I wasn't. I couldn't help seeing."

"You wouldn't have seen anything if I was rich."

"Why not?"

"Because then I'd wear panties. Now you'll have to take down your pants for me."

Srulik agreed. Marisza examined him and said, "Yours is different from the other boys'."

Srulik was frightened. He had forgotten that he mustn't take off his pants.

"Don't tell anyone," he said.

"I won't," Marisza promised.

Some days she didn't want to hunt. She just wanted to lie in the sun. She would give Srulik some hairs and let him hunt by himself while she kept an eye on his cows and sheep. He caught some birds, made a fire, and cooked them.

One day something strange happened to the fat cow. Although its udders had been swelling, Pani Nowek had said it wouldn't give milk until it calved. He wasn't sure what "calving" was. But now something was dropping from it. He was afraid that something was the matter and ran shouting to Marisza. She came to have a look and calmed him.

"She's just calving, you dope. Can't you see?"

Srulik couldn't believe his eyes when suddenly two little feet appeared. Marisza told him to grab hold of one of them. She seized the other and they began to pull. The cow bleated and panted. A mouth and muzzle appeared, and a minute later there was a head with eyes and ears. Srulik was flabbergasted. When the head was free, they gave a last pull and the baby calf popped out like a cork.

"What do I do now?" Srulik asked worriedly. "How do I get her home?"

"It's not a her, it's a him," Marisza said. "Don't worry. He'll walk by himself."

The other two cows came to have a look. One tried licking the calf, but the mother chased it away. Soon the calf struggled to its feet. It found its mother's teats and began to suck.

Srulik couldn't take his eyes off it. He had never seen anything so exciting.

"You never saw an animal give birth? Not even a dog or cat?"

"No. I once saw a baby goat in Blonie, but I didn't see it being born."

"You want to know something?"

Srulik looked at her curiously.

"You and I were born the same way."

He burst out laughing. "That's crazy."

"I'm telling you. That's why boys are made like you and girls like me."

He could see she was serious.

"Do you know how babies get into their mothers' stomachs?"

She told him.

"You really are crazy," he said.

"Didn't you ever see a dog mount a bitch? Or a billy-goat do it with a goat? When Pani Nowak takes her cow to the stud bull, you'll believe me."

"I know all that," Srulik said. "I saw dogs do it in Blonie. But people aren't dogs or cows."

Marisza shrugged. "You'll understand when you're older. At first I didn't want to believe it either."

✡

Every Sunday, Pani Nowek put on her best clothes and went to church. Sometimes, on her way out, she looked at Srulik as if wondering whether to take him too. But Sunday followed Sunday and she never did. Sometimes neighbors dropped by after church. Although Srulik tried to hide when they came, they sometimes spied him in the yard.

"I got him from my brother," the woman explained. "He's an orphan. His name is Jurek."

Some of the visitors smiled at him. One, an old woman, gave him nasty looks. Once he heard her ask Pani Nowek, "Barbara, why don't you bring him to church? Maybe he needs to be baptized."

"I'll talk to the priest," Pani Nowek said.

The conversation worried Srulik.

Something else worried him, too. And it was annoying. He had an itch that kept spreading. He didn't know if it was from dirt or lice. At first it was only on his hands. When he looked at his fingers, he saw what seemed like little white designs beneath the skin. Pani Nowek told him he had chiggers. It came, she said, from a tiny worm that burrowed into you.

"There's a salve for it," she said. "I'll ask the neighbors."

There wasn't enough time for her to get it, though.

One evening Srulik came back from the pasture and brought the cows to the barn for milking. Suddenly the dogs barked wildly and ran toward the road. A vehicle was approaching.

"The Germans are coming to confiscate livestock," Pani Nowek said angrily. "Run and hide in the storeroom. I'll shut the dogs up. Otherwise they'll shoot them."

Srulik ran to the storeroom and Pani Nowek grabbed the dogs and dragged them into the house. An army truck drove into the yard with two German soldiers. They produced a list and took a sheep from the shed. Srulik watched through a crack in the wooden door. It was his favorite sheep. A soldier lifted it onto the truck while the other headed with the woman for the barn. Srulik heard him ask, "Where's the Jewish boy?"

"I don't have any Jewish boy."

"In the village they say you do," the soldier said.

Srulik waited for them to enter the barn. Then he slipped from the storeroom, scaled the picket fence, and ran along the path leading past the potato field to the forest.

Just then, the second soldier stepped out of the barn with a cow on a rope. The cow gave the rope a yank and broke loose. The German cursed and ran after it. As he did, he spied Srulik. At first, he began to chase him. But seeing that the boy had too much of a head start, he ran back toward the truck, shouting to the first soldier to start driving toward him. The two of them set out in hot pursuit. But Srulik was nowhere in sight.

He wasn't in the forest yet. Hearing the truck, he knew

he had no time to reach it. He left the path, threw himself down in the potato field, and crawled among the plants.

The truck sped down the path and passed his hiding place. It reached some fallow ground between the field and the forest and stopped. A German jumped down, strode into the field, and began to search. He walked slowly, checking each row of potatoes. The driver switched off the engine and climbed onto the back of the truck to get a better view.

Srulik kept crawling toward the forest. He could see the branches of the trees without having to raise his head. He would get as close as he could and make a dash for them. He tried to move carefully, without touching the plants, thankful for every breeze that stirred them all at once. Something was blocking his way. He raised his head a bit and saw a man staring at him. The man was lying on the ground too. His hair was matted and wild and his lined, ashen face was covered with a growth of beard. Srulik realized he was a Jew like himself. He kept crawling until he was close enough to whisper:

"Get out of here! The Germans are after me."

The man didn't answer. His eyes widened in astonishment. He held out his arms and whispered back:

"Srulik . . ."

"Papa?"

Only now did he realize it was his father.

"I thought you and Mama had been killed," his father whispered.

"No."

"Where is she?"

"I don't know."

They could hear the two Germans shouting to each other. One voice was far away. The other was closer.

"Srulik, there's no time. I want you to remember what I'm going to tell you. You have to stay alive. You have to! Get someone to teach you how to act like a Christian, how to cross yourself and how to pray. Find a farmer you can stay with until the war ends. Always go to the poor people. They're more willing to help. And never swim in the river with other boys."

"I know that."

The German on the truck shouted to the German in the field. The German in the field was getting closer.

"We have no time," his father said. "If they come after you with dogs, find water or a swamp to cross. That throws them off the trail. And the most important thing, Srulik," he said, talking fast, "is to forget your name. Wipe it from your memory."

"I already have a Polish name," Srulik whispered. "It's Jurek."

"Good. From now on your name is Jurek Staniak. You remember Pani Staniak from the grocery in Blonie?"

"Yes, Papa."

"What's your name?"

"Jurek Staniak."

"But even if you forget everything—even if you forget me and Mama—never forget that you're a Jew."

"I won't, Papa."

His father stopped to think if he had left anything out. He said, "Always run to the forest. The Germans stay out of it because they're afraid of the partisans."

He listened to the footsteps of the approaching soldier. Then he pulled Srulik toward him, grasped his head with both hands, and kissed him while groaning like a wounded animal.

"Srulik, I'm going to run. The Germans will chase me. Count to ten slowly. Slowly, don't forget! Then run to the forest."

"All right, Papa."

His father jumped up and started to run. How much he had changed! The powerful man who could once lift a heavy sack of flour was now a shadow of himself. The two Germans let out a shout. Srulik forced himself to count, even though he wanted to run too. He counted slowly, as in a game of hide-and-seek. He reached ten, coiled himself, and sprang to his feet. From the corner of his eye he saw the two Germans chasing his father in the direction of the village. As fast as he could he ran the other way, toward the forest. Two shots rang out. Then another. He didn't turn to look. He ran until he was in the forest.

That night he couldn't fall asleep. Stretched out on the broad branch of a tree with his eyes shut, he kept seeing the potato field and his father. Now he saw every detail of his father's face. It had changed back again into the old face that he knew. He could concentrate on his father's words without having to hear the shouts of the Germans. You have to stay alive, Srulik. Get someone to teach you how to act like a Christian. Learn how to cross yourself. Always go to the poor people. Yes, Papa. Water throws the dogs off your trail. Forget your old name. You're

Jurek Staniak. But even if you forget me and Mama, never forget that you're a Jew. One two three four five six seven eight nine ten.

He fell asleep before hearing the shots, but they echoed in his dreams all night long. He kept running and running without looking back, the real face of his father in front of him.

7.

She's Going to Cook Me

Autumn came. The forest had a new look. The tree leaves turned yellow and began to fall. It grew harder to find berries to eat. He could still climb the trees for walnuts, but their shells were hard and had to be cracked with a stone. There were more and more mushrooms. He didn't recognize most of them and ate only the ones he knew from Blonie. The nice days were fewer. He was wet most of the time. Sometimes, as dusk approached, he slipped from the forest to steal food from a village. But the farmers, perhaps because of the approaching winter, now kept nearly everything under lock and key. Often, when he woke in the morning, the puddles of rainwater had a thin layer of ice. It was hard to pull the last carrots and radishes in the vegetable gardens from the frozen earth. The tomatoes and cucumbers were long gone. He was hungry and freezing.

Skirting a village one day, he saw an elderly farmer chopping wood, his jacket hanging on a fence post. After a while, the farmer put down his ax and entered his house. Srulik grabbed the jacket and ran. It was made of thick wool and had a lining. He shortened the sleeves with his piece of glass, found some rope, picked it apart, and tied the pieces of sleeve to his feet with the strands.

Sometimes he tried making a fire with Marisza's magnifying glass. It rarely worked. Either the sun didn't stay out long enough, or else it was too wet.

One night it began to snow. It was still snowing in the morning. Shivering from the cold, Srulik left the forest and went to look for work. It snowed all day. He plodded through the snow for hours until toward evening he reached a village half buried beneath a white blanket. A cold wind was blowing. There wasn't a soul in sight, not even a dog. Snow covered the houses, the thatch roofs, the bare treetops, the empty wagons in the farmyards, the wells and the fences. Narrow paths had been cleared by the doors of the houses. Srulik walked in the tracks of footprints that ran through the village. A pale light shone in some windows. He entered a farmyard, went to the hayloft, and fell asleep bundled in his jacket. His sleep was fitful. Now and then he awoke, shivering and feverish. He dreamed that he and his mother were in the clutches of the Gestapo. A stranger was pretending to be his father. He awoke in a fright. I'm sick, he thought. Always go to the poor people, Srulik, they're more willing to help. Yes, Papa.

When he opened his eyes in the morning, he didn't know where he was. His head hurt. He tried getting up and fell down. He crawled through the darkness toward the light from the door and pulled himself to his feet by leaning against the wall. The weather was gray and wintry. The farmyard didn't look especially poor. Although he wanted to knock on the door, he moved on.

It wasn't far from one farmhouse to the next. Yet the

distances seemed far greater than usual. Every step felt like his last. He had to force himself to pull his foot out of the snow and take another stride. His only desire was to lie down. Suddenly everything vanished and he saw only the gray sky. You have to stay alive, Srulik. Yes, Papa. He must have fallen. Mustering his will, he picked himself up. In front of him was a house with an old ruin next to it and a fence around part of a yard. These must be poor people, he thought. His vision grew blurred. He was seeing double. Rubbing his eyes, he made a supreme effort to climb the steps to the door. He knocked. And again. After a while, the door opened just a crack. Through the crack he made out a woman's face. She was the prettiest woman he had ever seen. Then everything went blank.

When he opened his eyes again, he was lying on a soft mattress. The pretty woman, who seemed to belong to some dream, was leaning over him. Above her was the ceiling of a house. Slowly he realized she was not a dream but the person who had opened the door. She was looking at him anxiously.

"You're awake?"

"Yes, ma'am."

The woman went over to a large pot on the fire. She's going to cook me and eat me, he thought.

She lifted the pot and poured hot water into a wooden tub. Then she undressed him and examined him. What will she do to me now? he thought helplessly. Shaking her head, she examined his sores and put him in the tub. The water was very hot and he yelled. She scrubbed him thoroughly without sparing the soap. Then she took him from the tub, dried him, laid him in front of the stove, and smeared his body with a black salve. His sores hurt. He moaned and groaned.

The woman went off for a while. When she came back she moved his mattress closer to the stove and added wood to the fire.

Now she'll throw me into it, Srulik thought.

But she merely covered him with a blanket. Though his whole body was smarting, he fell asleep with a hopeful feeling.

That feeling was justified. In the days to come the woman took care of him devotedly and Srulik recovered his strength. She gave him good, warm clothes to wear.

"What did you do with my old ones?" he asked.

"I threw them out."

He grieved for them until she took down Marisza's magnifying glass from a mantel and gave it to him.

✡

Christmastime came. Srulik could already say the Catholic prayers. He never touched his food until the pretty woman had said grace and he had crossed himself. Around his neck she had hung a cross and a medallion of the Madonna holding baby Jesus. One day she brought him a pair of shoes.

They were big for him. She stuffed them with newspaper.

"That's what my mother used to do," Srulik said.

"Don't tell me anything about yourself," she told him. "It's better for me not to know. Just tell me how old you are."

He thought for a moment.

"I was eight last summer," he said.

"What should I call you?"

"Jurek Staniak."

"That's a fine name," the woman said.

She wouldn't let him go near the windows during the day. At night, after she lit the kerosene lamp in the main room, he had to stay in an alcove in the back. It was dark there and the windows were covered by thick curtains.

"Why?" he asked.

At first she wouldn't tell him. Then she did.

"I have two sons in the partisans. Do you know what that is?"

He nodded.

"I had a daughter, too, but the Germans tortured her and hung her in the forest. She couldn't have told where her father and brothers were even if she had wanted to. She didn't know."

Her eyes were dry as she told him this. Her face was pale and severe.

"I think they've left me here as bait. They keep me under surveillance to see who visits me. That's why I have to hide you. It's too dangerous to run the risk of going out or being seen through a window. And at night, when the lamp is lit, you could be spotted even more easily. I'm afraid that you won't be able to stay here. If the Germans come looking for my husband or sons, they may kill you."

She opened a trapdoor in the kitchen. A ladder led down from it to a basement full of vegetables. "Meanwhile, if anything happens I'll hide you here," she said.

He helped her to decorate the little Christmas tree she brought home. On Christmas Eve she lit some candles on the tree. He watched from the door of his alcove as she

71

knelt and prayed, beating her breast.

The next day she gave him a hat. He took fright.

"Don't worry," she said. "I'm not sending you away just yet."

She told him to go to his alcove, shut the door, and knock. When she opened it, he was to enter the big room, take off his hat, and say, "Blessed be Jesus Christ." Then he would wait for her to answer, "Forever and ever, amen." They practiced it a few times.

Finally she said, "Very good. And what will you say when you're asked where you're from and who your parents are? You have to be prepared."

"I don't know."

She sat him down in front of her and told him, "You were born in a little village. You don't remember its name. You don't know how old you are. All you remember is that one day your father hitched the horses to the wagon, loaded all your belongings on it, and set out with you and your mother."

"I don't have brothers or sisters?"

"No. You're an only child."

"I used to be the youngest," he said.

"The three of you set out. The road was full of wagons, horses, cars, and soldiers. You don't remember how long you traveled. All of a sudden you heard a loud noise. A plane flew over you very low, on a strafing run. Bullets hit your wagon and your horse. Your parents fell and didn't move. They didn't answer when you called to them. Their clothes were sticky and red. Some people took you to their village. You don't remember how long you were there. But the man got drunk and beat you, so you left. Since then you've drifted from place to place. Can you remember all that?"

"No."

Every day she repeated the story to him. He didn't have to remember it exactly as she told it, she said. He just had to know some version of it by heart. When he was asked about himself, he had to tell as if it were true.

One day she asked without warning, "Where are you from?"

"I don't remember."

"Where are you parents?"

"They were killed when a plane strafed our wagon."

"How old are you?"

"I guess I'm nine."

"Very good," she praised him. "Now I'll teach you what to do when the people you work for take you to church."

"What people?"

"Whoever."

She explained what he should do when entering the church and leaving it. During the service, he should imitate the others.

A few days later, she woke him one morning and told him the time had come. He had to go to another village, because his presence might already have been detected. During the night she had heard voices and footsteps outside the house. She sewed the sleeves of the wool jacket that he had shortened and helped him into it, even though he could do it by himself. Then she handed him a bag with some provisions and said, "If you're ever in bad trouble, you can always come back to me. And if you can't get here, go to a church and ask the priest for help." She regarded him. "You're an enchanting child, Jurek. People will always help you."

He looked at the pretty woman. She didn't look so poor to him. She just looked very sad and lonely. Maybe, he thought, sad, lonely people could be trusted just like poor ones.

The weeks of living with her had made him strong and healthy. He had even put on weight. Setting out into the snowy world that morning, he felt not only better physically, but more confident. He now knew what to do and how to behave. He wasn't Srulik anymore. He was Jurek Staniak. He touched the cross and the Madonna around his neck, as if to verify this.

The villages were not far apart. A few kilometers was all that lay between them. Two or three hours of walking in the snow brought him to the next one. This time he didn't go looking for a hovel at the village's end. He picked the biggest, wealthiest-looking farmhouse and knocked on the door. It opened. A wave of warmth from the heat inside enveloped him. Jurek Staniak took off his hat and said in a clear voice:

"Blessed be Jesus Christ."

The expected answer came at once. He was invited to come in.

8.

Jesus Was a Jew, Too

The Wrubels were eating at the kitchen table. Pan Wrubel invited him to join them. Pani Wrubel filled a dish with potatoes and an omelet. Jurek remembered to cross himself before beginning to eat. The meal passed in silence, apart from the sounds of lips smacking and spoons clinking against tin plates. Jurek glanced at the plate of the light-haired boy sitting next to him. It had pieces of meat on it.

When they were through eating, Pan Wrubel turned to him and asked, "What brings you here, son?"

"I'm looking for work."

"What's your name?"

"Jurek Staniak."

"What can you do?"

"Anything."

"Where are you from?"

Jurek shrugged.

"How come you don't know?"

He told them how a plane had strafed their wagon.

"Papa and Mama just lay there. They didn't talk. The horse was dead. At first some people took me to their village. But the man beat me, so I left. Since then I've been on the move. If someone beats me, I go somewhere else."

"You poor orphan," Pani Wrubel said.

"You must have been heading east to get away from the Germans," Pan Wrubel remarked.

Jurek nodded. "I guess so," he said.

"You poor orphan," Pani Wrubel repeated.

"I'll take you on," said Pan Wrubel. "You can sleep in the barn or the sheep shed. We'll give you your meals."

Mateusz Wrubel was a big, fat, bald man. His wife Mania was thin and stooped, with a wrinkled face and the hands of someone who had worked all her life. The light-haired boy seemed to be about twelve. A young man sitting next to him looked like his brother.

At first, Jurek's only work was taking care of the pigs. He didn't mind it at all. They were fed a flour and potato mash that he often ate himself. After a while he was also given the chore of feeding the cows before milking, and the sheep if there was no one else to do it. The horses were reserved for Pan Wrubel and his eldest son. Jurek was afraid of horses. At the same time, however, he admired them and never missed a chance to step into the stable and pet them. Ever since the farmer outside the Warsaw ghetto had abandoned the wagon and sped off with him on his horse, he had felt grateful to horses. The memory of the big, warm body with its short, silky hair galloping beneath him had stayed with him.

One day, noticing how he looked at the horses, Franek, the teenage boy, asked, "Would you like me to teach you to ride?"

"Yes," Jurek said.

"I'll let you know the next time I wash the horses,"

Franek said. "That's a good time."

✡

One day Pan Wrubel came to watch him at work and nodded with satisfaction.

"How old are you?" he asked.

"I guess nine."

"So if I beat you you'll go somewhere else?"

Jurek grinned.

"When I was your age, I was sent away to work for the
local squire. I only came home on Sundays. We were ten
children. Whenever a new one was born, someone had to
leave home to make room."

He told Jurek about all the cows, sheep, and horses he
had owned before the Germans came and took them.

All week long Pan Wrubel was friendly. He slapped
Jurek on the back and was kind to all of his animals, not
just the horses. But on Sundays, when he came home
drunk, he was a terror. Usually, he spent Saturday nights
drinking with his friends until dawn. Everyone knew he
was home because of the shouts, screams, and sounds of
dishes breaking and doors banging. If his eldest son
Viktor was there, he defended his mother. Pan Wrubel
would have to leave the house and take out his anger on
the animals, kicking the cows and chasing the pigs around
their sty. If he caught Franek or Jurek, he slapped their
faces, pulled their ears, and marched them in front of him
with kicks in the rear. Monday mornings found him pen-
itent and unshaven. Still dressed in his creased weekend
clothes, he would look for Jurek and ask, "Say, how many
times did I hit you yesterday?"

Jurek would present him with the bill and receive a one-zloty coin for every time. It was enough to buy candy in the village store and sometimes a box of matches. He remembered being without matches in the forest and decided to hoard them.

One Monday, Franek heard his father ask Jurek the usual question. When Pan Wrubel walked off, he said, "Are you a dope! Why don't you add a few more slaps? That's what I do. I'd run away from home if he didn't pay me for hitting me, but this way it's worth it."

The two of them went to the village store to buy candy. Pani Wrubel saw them returning together. "You see, Franek," she said. "You always wanted a little brother. Now you have one." She turned to Jurek. "Why don't you ever go to play with the village boys?"

"Where?"

"Franek will show you."

Franek led Jurek to an empty lot behind the last house of the village. In summer it served as a soccer field. Now a circle of boys, ranging in age from tots to teenagers, was standing around two youngsters fighting with whips. They lashed at each other with a savage fury. Jurek had never seen such a sport. He and Franek joined the circle. The whip fight went on until one boy surrendered. Now, everyone turned to look at Jurek.

"Who's that?"

"He works for us," Franek said.

"Come on, we'll see what you're made of," someone said.

At first Jurek feared he would have to take part in a whip fight. But to join the gang of boys, it turned out, you only had to wrestle. A boy was chosen who seemed a fair match for him. Jurek pinned him easily. Then he had to fight a bigger boy. They wrestled for a long time, rolling on the ground to the cheers of the other boys. At first everyone except Franek cheered for Jurek's rival. Gradually, though, Jurek's grit won him sympathy. In the end it was decided to call it a draw.

From then on, Jurek went to play with the village boys. Sometimes Franek came too. Jurek excelled at rag-ball soccer and tried to stay out of whip fights, though he took part in them when he had to. There were also spitting and peeing contests. Spitting was no problem. In peeing, though, he had to be careful to let no one see that he was circumcised. Fortunately, everyone was looking at where the pee landed. And at running Jurek was the champion. No one was faster.

"I'll bring my big brother tomorrow," a boy said. "Let's see you beat him."

The next day the boy brought his brother. A starting and finish line were drawn and everyone watched tensely. A whistle served as the starting gun. Jurek won. The older brother, humiliated, kicked him.

"You dirty Yid!" he said.

Franek and his friends didn't like that. "Watch it, Zygmunt," Franek said. "Call him a Yid again and I'll have my brother kick your ass."

Zygmunt cursed and walked off. But he didn't forget the insult.

When spring came and Pan Wrubel and his two sons were busy with the plowing and sowing, Jurek was given the job of taking the cows out to pasture. For the first few days, Franek went with him. He showed Jurek his slingshot and demonstrated his skill with it, killing two grouse in no time.

Jurek gathered wood and arranged it for a fire. Franek took one look at it, scattered it with a kick, and looked at it scornfully.

"Come here, you idiot," he said. "I'll teach you how to do it."

He went to the nearby woods and came back with some twigs, some dry pine needles, and a few larger branches. Building a well-aired structure of the twigs, he put the pine needles beneath them and lit them with matches. Once the flames took hold, he added the branches. Soon they had a merry bonfire. Jurek brought mud from the next field and they baked the grouse as village boys have always done.

"Franek, how do I make a slingshot?" Jurek asked.

"I'll sell you this one," Franek said. "I've got two more at home."

"How much do you want for it?"

"Ten zloty. You can earn them back in two or three Sundays."

Jurek was thrilled to have his own slingshot. He practiced constantly, aiming at whatever did or didn't move—for the time being, without much success.

Franek remembered his promise. One hot day he invited Jurek to come with him and the horses to the stream.

"Bareback?" Jurek marveled, looking at the unsaddled horses.

"What did you think?" Franek said. "You don't wash a horse with its saddle. Come on, I'll help you up. The spotted mare is easy to ride."

Jurek sat on the spotted horse, looking for something to grab onto.

"Hold on to its mane," Franek said.

He mounted the other horse with a third in tow and they set out. Once Jurek got over his fear of swaying so high off the ground, he was joyful.

They reached the stream. The horses were happy to be in the water and frisked about in it. Jurek and Franek waded in after them and Franek took some rags from his pocket.

"Rub her down well," he told Jurek, pointing to the mare. "She likes it."

It was hard work. But when the two of them rode back into the village on the horses, Jurek felt full of pride.

From now on Pan Wrubel would sometimes let him ride the spotted mare to pasture. He rode her bareback, with a bit and reins to help control her.

He still hadn't managed to hunt a grouse with Franek's slingshot. Meanwhile, he hunted smaller birds with a horsehair. Each time he set a trap for them he thought of Marisza—of her braids and her dress and her fingers tossing the jacks. Do you know why I'm nice to you? Thinking of those words gave him a good feeling.

But Zygmunt still had it in for him. He was just waiting for a chance to get even. One day he stopped to watch a peeing contest. Jurek stood in the line of waiting boys and didn't notice him. Before he knew it Zygmunt came over and grabbed his hands, baring his penis.

"I knew it!" he crowed. "I knew it! You're a Yid. Now you'll come with me. The Germans will be happy to have you."

Jurek squirmed from his grasp and ran off. Zygmunt chased him but soon gave up and went to get his father.

Jurek ran back to the house. Pan Wrubel and his sons were outside, fixing a wagon. Jurek told them what had happened.

"Zygmunt?" Viktor said. "That's what you might expect of someone from his family."

"You lied to us," Pan Wrubel told Jurik. "You put us all in danger."

Franek defended him. "He had no choice."

"You be quiet!"

"Franek's right," Viktor said.

"What's the matter, wasn't he a good worker?" Franek asked. "Are you going to turn him over to the Germans just because of Zygmunt's family?"

"No," his father said. "You're right, Franek. Call your mother."

Jurek went to the barn to get his jacket and his knapsack. In it were the shoes the pretty woman had given him.

Pani Wrubel was waiting for him when he returned. She had some food that she put into his knapsack.

"May Jesus Christ watch over you Jurek," she said.

"Of course he will," said Viktor. "He was a Jew, too."

Pan Wrubel threw his hammer down on the wagon. "You sinner!" he shouted angrily. "How dare you talk like that? You'll go to hell!"

"I'll meet you there, Papa," Viktor said.

"Stop it," Pani Wrubel begged. "Say goodbye to the boy. He's just a poor orphan."

Franek and Viktor walked him past the last house of the village. They were afraid Zygmunt and his father might waylay him along the road. Jurek turned around and watched them walk back. He looked sadly at the houses of the village. He had thought that he had at last found a farmer to stay with until the end of the war.

9.

A True Friend

Jurek found his next family by accident. He had stepped
out of the forest to look on the road for some stones for
his slingshot. A farmer was sowing in his field, reaching
into the sack on his shoulder and casting the golden seeds
with a broad, regular movement as if doing the Lord's
work. Fascinated, Jurek walked closer for a better look. It
was lunchtime. A woman came from the village to bring
the farmer food. Jurek stepped up to them and greeted
them.

"Are you hungry, boy?"

He nodded.

"Help yourself," the farmer said.

He crossed himself and sat down with them to eat. After
putting a few questions to him, the woman turned to her
husband and said, "Jozef Wapielnik is looking for a
cowherd. Shall I take the boy with me to the village?"

The farmer nodded.

Jurek went with the farmer's wife. The village nestled at
the foot of a small hill. On the hilltop were the ruins of an
impressively large building, an old fortress or perhaps a
castle. The woman brought him to a big, well-maintained

farmhouse and knocked on the door. A somber-looking farmer opened it.

"You've been looking for a new cowherd," the woman said. "I've brought you one."

Pan Wapielnik surveyed him. "All right," he said. "I'll try him out. What's your name?"

"Jurek Staniak."

Jurek was told to wait in the yard. Pan Wapielnik went and brought a wheelbarrow full of food for the pigs and sent Jurek to feed them. When he was done, he found the farmer sitting in front of his house.

"You can sleep in the hayloft," he told Jurek. "Tomorrow you'll take the cows to pasture."

"Yes, sir."

Pan Wapielnik took him to the hayloft and pointed to a blanket in a corner. Someone had bedded down here before him. Shaking the blanket to air it, he heard something fall. He bent down and picked up a pocket knife. He opened it. It had only one blade, the tip of which was broken. He recognized it at once. It was Yosele's. Was he the cowherd here before him? What had happened to him? He didn't dare ask Pan Wapielnik. Perhaps eventually he would.

Jozef Wapielnik was an irritable man. His small, unattractive wife was always busy. They had three grown daughters. Two worked on the farm and helped their mother with the milking. The youngest and prettiest lived in another village and sometimes visited on Sundays. There were also two younger children smaller than Jurek, a boy and a girl. Pan Wapielnik took both of them every morning on horseback to their school in a nearby town.

The next day he rode his horse alongside Jurek to the pasture. His herd numbered more than fifteen cows and Jurek had to run around a lot to keep them all in the meadow. Once the farmer saw that he knew what to do, he left him alone with them. At least twice a day, however, he came by to make sure that his cows were all right.

One day a cow calved in the meadow. Jurek knew exactly what to do. When Pan Wapielnik arrived, he received a nod of approval—the highest praise the farmer ever gave. Pan Wapielnik put the calf on his horse and rode home with the bleating mother behind him.

Jurek didn't play with the village boys. If he wasn't given extra chores after coming home with the cows, he stayed on the farm and played with his dog, a big, black-and-white spotted mongrel with a black ring around one eye, which had turned up one day. Jurek took to feeding it and the dog came to sleep with him at night in the hayloft. One morning, while he was letting the cows out of their milking stalls, one of them stepped on the dog's front foot.

The foot was broken. Pan Wapielnik went to get an ax with which to put the dog out of its misery, but Jurek carried the dog to the hayloft. He straightened the broken leg and made a splint from two pieces of wood tied with strips of cotton. The dog couldn't walk. Jurek went on feeding it and sleeping with it at night. Sometimes he brought it milk from the barn. He called it Azor.

For many days Azor hardly moved. Then he began to hobble with his bad leg in the air and tried to work the splint off. Jurek scolded him and tied it back in place. A few weeks went by. When the foot had mended enough for Azor to use it, Jurek took off the splint and massaged it. The dog walked on all four legs again, although with a limp.

Azor became Jurek's best friend and went with him everywhere. One day the farmer, who had forgotten about the incident, saw the two of them together and asked with surprise, "Where is that dog from?"

"It's the dog you wanted to kill, Pan Jozef," Jurek said.

"It limps a bit, eh? That's no reason why it can't make a good guard dog."

That night, he tied Azor with a chain outside the house. In the morning, he let Jurek free him. Only on Sundays did Azor remain chained all day. That was when Pan Wapielnik had visitors. He was proud of his big new guard dog and wanted to show him off.

Jurek's new employers never invited him into their house. After coming home with the cows, he would be brought his supper by one of the girls. Usually this was a bowl of noodles and vegetables or potatoes mashed with lard and onions. On Sundays he was given an omelet with sausage. He was hungry all the time. Although he knew Pan Wapielnik wouldn't like it if he took his mind off the cows, one day he couldn't resist hunting a grouse with his slingshot. As soon as the farmer departed after one of his visits, Jurek made a fire and put the grouse in the coals. As luck would have it, Pan Wapielnik returned unexpectedly soon afterward. Finding Jurek by the fire, he stuck him hard with his whip.

"I've got a big herd," he said. "If I ever catch you sitting by a fire again, I'll sack you at once."

"Yes, Pan Jozef."

After the farmer was gone, Jurek ate the cooked grouse. But he didn't dare hunt anymore.

✡

It was high spring. One fine Sunday morning Jurek lay in the meadow playing one of his favorite games. Taking off his shirt, he hung it on a board in the sun and waited for the lice to leave it. Then, with the help of a stem, he forced them to walk in a straight line. Any louse breaking ranks was squashed at once.

After a while, he laid his head on the ground and fell asleep. Azor was chained up and wasn't with him.

He awoke to a stinging pain. Jozef Wapielnik was standing beside his horse and whipping him. Jurek leaped to his feet. The cows were grazing in a field of carrots. Before Jurek could run toward them the farmer seized him and bound his hands with the whip. He was unsteady on his feet and stank of alcohol. Twice he tried mounting his horse and fell off. The third time he succeeded, dragging Jurek after him. Jurek's knapsack and jacket, all the property he owned in the world, remained in the meadow.

"Pan Jozef, the cows!" Jurek shouted. But the farmer paid him no attention. He simply mumbled to himself and uttered a string of curses. When they reached the farmyard, he dismounted, or rather, fell off his horse, freed Jurek's hands, grabbed him by the hair, and began to beat him with the handle of the whip. Jurek screamed. Azor fought to come to the rescue. On his third leap he broke the chain and pounced on the farmer. Pan Wapielnik let go of Jurek and tumbled to the ground, trying to protect himself with the whip.

"Azor, come!" Jurek called in a fright, afraid the dog would murder the man. He began to run. Azor left Pan Wapielnik and ran after him.

He returned to the meadow, gathered his things, and headed for the forest. As soon as he entered the dark cover of the trees, he felt like someone returning to a hometown whose streets and lanes he knew by heart. And now he had a friend with him.

The first night, Jurek reverted to his old custom of sleeping in a tree. But Azor soon began to whimper and he climbed down and lay beside him on a mattress of pine needles. His thoughts turned to Yosele and his knife. Had Yosele also run away because Pan Wapielnik beat him? He would never know.

He fell asleep and dreamed that something was rolling on him and choking him. He wanted to ask his brother to help him but couldn't remember his name. Although it was on the tip of his tongue he couldn't think of it. And when he shouted, his brother didn't recognize his voice and walked away. He knew he would come to him if called by name, but the name continued to escape him. He woke up breathing heavily.

Azor was lying on his chest, licking him. Jurek sat up and stroked the dog's head. It was wet. Jurek licked his lips. He was thirsty.

"Did you find water?" he asked.

Azor wagged his tail. Jurek listened to the forest. There was a sound of running water. He went to look for the brook that was making it. It made him think of his first day in the forest with the Jewish boys. How long ago had that been? He tried to calculate. Since then a whole winter and spring had gone by and it was almost summer again.

He went to pick berries for his breakfast. Azor didn't know what to make of them. He ate some and spit out others. Jurek burst out laughing and hugged him. "You'd rather have meat, wouldn't you?" he said.

Azor cocked his head as though deliberating. Jurek took out his slingshot and strode off purposefully through the trees. A bird took off from a branch, sensing danger. But practice had made perfect and he brought the wood pigeon down. It fell to the ground with a broken wing and made for the bushes. Azor pounced on it.

"Fetch, Azor!" he ordered as he had done in their games.

The dog gave him a sly look.

He raised his voice. "Azor!"

The dog obeyed and brought him the bird. There was not enough meat on it for the two of them.

"Still," he said to Azor, giving him the innards and bones, "it's better than nothing."

They were still eating when he spied another wood pigeon, perhaps the first one's mate. He downed it too. Now they could eat to their hearts' content.

The next day Azor disappeared in the undergrowth, came back, and was gone again. Jurek listened and heard an odd sound, as if of branches being shaken. Following Azor, he discovered a rabbit dangling by its foot from a slipknot. Opening the knot, he removed it from the rabbit's foot. The animal screeched horridly. Jurek was afraid the sound might bring the forester or the trapper, if not worse. The rabbit had to be killed quickly. He did it with his eyes shut and moved away through the forest to be safe. This time, he waited until nighttime to make a fire. He cut the rabbit into pieces and roasted them on a spit. Azor ate too. It was a royal feast and there was enough left over for the next day.

Jurek became a good hunter. He bagged a small rabbit, a squirrel, and once, after several misses, a large duck swimming in a reed-encircled pond.

"Azor, fetch!" he called.

The dog jumped into the water at once and fetched the duck. There was enough meat for three days.

Another time, Jurek killed and cooked a blue jay. But its meat was inedible. It was tough and had a bad smell. He gave it to Azor, who didn't think much of it either.

They weren't alone in the forest. A growl from Azor would warn him when there were people or wild boar around. Grabbing the dog and pinching his jaws shut with both hands, Jurek would whisper:

"Shhhhh!"

And Azor would hush up. After each such near encounter—with what or whom only Azor knew—they hid for a while in the bushes. At night Jurek lay with his arms around the dog, making sure he didn't bark. Sometimes, hearing low voices or footsteps, he guessed that partisans were near. He debated letting them know he was there. But Yosele had said they wanted no part of Jewish boys.

And then disaster struck. It was a clear day. Toward noon he heard voices and people running. Before he could grab Azor and slip away, a large dog bounded toward them, foaming at the mouth. Two men with rifles ran after it. They shouted when they saw him, "Mad dog! Run, boy!"

Jurek ran as fast as he could. Azor ran after him, bounding over a large fallen tree. Jurek felt a sharp pain in his heel. He ignored it and kept running. The mad dog was gaining on them. He halted, grabbed a large branch, and swung around to face the beast. Azor bared his fangs and threw himself at the attacker. Jurek tried striking the rabid dog on the head, not realizing what danger he was in. The two men came running up.

"Get out of the way, boy!"

Jurek jumped aside. Two shots rang out.

"No!" Jurek cried. "No!"

They fired two more shots. The mad dog was dead. Azor lay dying.

Jurek slumped to the ground in pain, hugging his dog. He didn't cry. One of the men stroked his head. He pushed the hand angrily away. The man said, "Son, your dog saved your life."

"But what did you kill him for?"

"Look. We had to kill them both. When a man or dog is bitten by an animal with rabies, they get it too and die a horrible death. Do you understand? Look how your dog has bites all over."

Jurek nodded.

"Where are you from?"

"The village." He pointed vaguely.

"Over there?" They looked in the direction he had pointed in. "There's no village there. You're confused. You must mean there." They pointed somewhere else.

Jurek nodded.

The two men talked things over and decided to burn the dead dogs. One went to gather pine needles, and the other, dry branches. Jurek tried helping them, but he couldn't step on his injured foot.

"What happened to you?" one of the men asked.

Jurek sat down and looked at his heel. "I must have landed on something when I jumped," he said.

He overcame his pain and lent a hand. The men looked tense and nervous.

"Would you stay here and watch the fire?" one asked him. "Here, here's ten zloty. We have to go. If any animal eats the carcass before it's burned, the rabies will spread. Do you understand?"

Jurek understood. He didn't take the money. "All right," he said.

He sat and watched the fire. The smoke burned his eyes. Tears ran from them.

Someone was standing there. Jurek looked up. The man lifted an arm to hit him. When he saw what was burning, though, he checked himself. It was a forester, a different one from the one Jurek knew.

"What are you doing?" he asked.

Jurek told him.

"Two men with rifles, you say?"

"Yes."

"Not Germans? Not police?"

"No."

The forester nodded thoughtfully. He asked, "Where are you from?"

This time Jurek pointed in the right direction.

"Go home," the forester said. "I don't want you burning down this forest. I'll take care of the fire myself."

That night Jurek went back to sleeping in the trees. He tied himself to a branch with his rope belt and dreamed of Azor. In his dream Azor could climb trees and was lying next to him. Then Azor turned into his brother. They were sleeping together in one bed. But his brother slept badly and kept kicking him in the foot.

Jurek awoke. Dawn was breaking. The forest floor beneath him was still dark. His foot felt worse. By evening he could hardly walk. Two more days went by and his heel swelled and turned yellow with pus. The skin was too callused to pierce with a pine needle and he was afraid to cut it with Yosele's knife. He needed help. Breaking off a branch to use as a walking stick, he hobbled in the direction the two armed men had pointed in. When he came to the village, he remembered the pretty woman's advice and headed for the spire of the church. Next to it was a house, and he knocked on the door. An old priest opened it. Jurek greeted him in the name of Jesus. The priest reached out to pat his head and he kissed the priest's hand as he had seen people do in village streets.

"You're not from here," the priest said.

"No, Father."

"Where are you from?"

"I have no parents. I just go from place to place."

"What can I do for you, my son?"

Jurek showed the priest his foot. The priest looked at the swollen heel and told Jurek to come in. He went to a closet, took a razor blade, and cut the thick skin on Jurek's heel. Then he squeezed out the pus, wiped it away with a clean rag, and pulled out a long splinter. Finally, he smeared salve on the heel and bandaged it.

"Martha," he called. "Bring some bread and milk. We have a young guest."

A middle-aged woman entered the room and put on the table a large glass of milk and a plate with two thick slices of bread and lard. Jurek reached for it, remembered in time to cross himself, and began to eat. Although he tried eating slowly and politely, it wasn't easy.

The priest sat watching him. From time to time he shook his head and smiled.

"How old are you, my son?"

"About nine," Jurek said.

The priest asked the usual questions. Jurek answered them. When he was done eating, he asked, "Does anyone around here need a boy to do some work?"

"Try the big house. Come, I'll show you where it is."

The priest walked him to the churchyard. "Just follow this street," he said. "And if you stay in the village, come back and see me again."

"I will, Father."

The priest blessed him and Jurek limped off, leaning on his stick. A group of boys was playing rag soccer in the street. He would have joined them if not for his foot. They stopped their game to watch him go by. He heard a boy say, "See that blond kid? I know him. He used to play with us when I visited my cousins."

The boy added something in a whisper.

"Go on!" said a second boy. "I just saw him come from the priest."

"I'm telling you it's true," the first boy insisted.

Jurek kept walking without hastening his stride. When he reached the end of the village, he continued as fast as his foot allowed him to. Now and then he turned around to look. No one was following him.

He had never heard anyone call him "that blond kid" before. He had always been "Red." The sun had bleached his hair without his knowing it.

10.

Do You Smoke?

Jurek realized that he was known by too many people in the area. He decided to cross the Wisla River and try his luck elsewhere. As soon as his foot was better, he left the forest and set out. A wagon loaded with sacks of wheat passed on the road. A farmer and his wife were sitting in the front seat. Jurek greeted them and asked if they were traveling toward the Wisla.

"Yes. To the flour mill."

"Can you give me a ride?"

The farmer's wife looked at him and whispered something to her husband.

"Hop aboard," the farmer said.

Jurek climbed onto the wagon and lay on the sacks, which were growing warm in the morning sun. The wagon jolted slowly along the cobblestone road, and he fell asleep.

He awoke and opened his eyes when the wagon came to a halt. He wasn't at a flour mill. There were no waterwheels and no river. He was in the yard of a large, three-story house with pretty trimmings. Surrounding it and several nearby structures was a metal fence topped by barbed wire. The wire pointed outward, against intruders.

Jurek had never seen such a fence around a village house. But it was too late to do anything about it. The gate had swung shut and was guarded by a German soldier.

He was at the local headquarters of the Gestapo.

The farmer brought him into the house. A soldier shut the door behind them. The farmer let go of Jurek and stepped into an office. The soldier pointed to a kitchen and told Jurek in German to go there. A Polish woman was working in the kitchen. Without a word, she sat Jurek at a table and gave him a large bowl of meat and rice. He crossed himself and ate hungrily, finishing it all. Then he leaned back with a contented sigh.

"That was a serving for two grown men," the woman said, laughing and taking the empty bowl.

Jurek rose and went to the window. The forest was near.

"Is there a road leading to the forest, ma'am?" he asked.

The cook pointed out the window. "Do you see that wooden shack? The path to the forest is behind it."

He peeked into the corridor to see if he could make a getaway. The soldier at the door spotted him. Grabbing Jurek's arm, he pulled him down some stairs and locked him in a basement. The basement was ankle-high in water. Some broken wooden crates were afloat in it. Jurek sat on one of them. After a long while the door opened and the soldier told him to come out. He led him upstairs and knocked on a door. "Come in!" said a voice in German.

The soldier ushered Jurek into the room, saluted, and left.

The room was a large one. A young, blond, handsome officer was sitting behind a long table. His uniform brimmed with decorations. Beneath the German eagle and the swastika on his officer's cap, which was placed on the table, was the insignia of a skull. A large photograph of Hitler hung on a wall. The officer gave the barefoot child in tattered clothes a bored look. He went over to him and asked in broken Polish, "What's your name?"

"Jurek Staniak."

"Are you a Jew?"

"No."

The German gave him a slap.

"Where do you live?"

"Wherever there's work."

"Where are your parents?"

"They were killed when the war broke out."

"How?"

Jurek told his story.

"And since then you've been on your own?"

"No. At first a couple took me to their village. But the husband got drunk and beat me, and I ran away. I don't stick around if I'm beaten."

"How old are you?"

"About nine."

"And when were you last beaten?"

"Just now. By you."

The German laughed.

"I don't mean just one slap."

"A month ago."

"Why?"

"Because the cows got into the carrots."

"And you ran away?"

"Yes. To the forest, with my dog."

"You had a dog?"

"Yes."

"Where is it?"

"Some farmers killed it because a mad dog bit it."
Jurek wiped his nose.

"How?"

"They shot it."

"They did?" The German raised his brows. "Where was that?"

Jurek shrugged.

"I don't know. In the forest."

"Are you a Jew?"

"No."

"Can you cross yourself?"

He crossed himself.

"Can you pray?"

Jurek said the prayers he had learned.

"I'm afraid I don't believe you," the German said. "Take off your clothes."

Jurek undressed, covering his private parts with his hands. The German rapped his hands with a ruler. Jurek dropped them and the German said:

"What's this?"

"I was operated on because of an infection."

"No, you weren't. Only Jews have that."

The German slapped him hard.

"I'm not a Jew," Jurek insisted.

"All right, get dressed," the officer said.

Jurek dressed.

"You're a smart kid," said the German. "It's too bad you're Jewish. Come with me."

The officer led him through the door and into the yard. He walked up and down there with Jurek at his side. Pulling out a gold case, he took a cigarette and offered one to Jurek.

"Do you smoke?"

"No."

The German lit the cigarette. They resumed walking up and down in silence. From time to time the German puffed on his cigarette and blew out smoke. Jurek saw his right hand steal toward the pistol in his holster. Like an arrow from a bow, he took off for the back of the wooden shack. But he hadn't understood the woman in the kitchen. Although there was a path to the forest, it was on the other side of the fence. Jurek didn't slow down when he reached the fence. He just kept running right up it, scaling it like a wild animal. The first two shots rang out when he had reached the top. One whistled past his ear. The other grazed his shoulder. He vaulted the barbed wire, fell to the ground on the other side, and got to his feet and ran some more. There were three more shots. He heard a motorcycle and the barking of dogs. Turning around to look, he saw a cycle bumping over the field. Two Germans on horseback, dogs loping at their sides, were closer to him.

He was already in the forest, pumping his long legs as fast as they would go. From somewhere came a swampy smell. He ran toward it, remembering what his father had told him. Suddenly his legs were sinking into mud. He ran on until he could no longer pull them out of it. Then he grabbed hold of a low-hanging branch and lay down flat.

He could feel his body sinking slowly into quicksand. Soon only his head and his hands gripping the branch were above the surface.

The dogs reached the swamp. They stopped at the edge of it and went off in another direction. After them came the two soldiers on horseback. Jurek could tell from their shouts and curses that their horses were deep in mud too. For a long time afterward, he heard them calling to the dogs.

He pulled himself up by the branch. It creaked and he was afraid it would break. Slowly he managed to extricate himself. Then he crawled forward on his stomach, holding on to the bushes.

11.
Ration Tickets

Jurek spent the next few weeks in the forest. One day he left it, walked to a village, and sneaked into a farmyard in the hope of finding some cheese or a chicken. A farmer stepping out of his outhouse caught hold of Jurek with one hand while the other was still buttoning his pants.

"What are you doing here?"

Jurek kept his wits about him.

"I'm looking for work."

"Good," the farmer said. "My oldest son has a job in town and the little ones are too small. I need a cowherd."

Jurek liked the looks of the man. He liked his wife too, a fat, smiling woman. After a few days his new employer asked him to come with him to the mayor of the village.

"The times are hard," he said. "The Germans confiscate everything. What they allow you to keep depends on the number of heads in the family. And you," he said, laughing, "have a head."

"But why are we taking the wagon?" Jurek asked.

"Because after the mayor fills out a form, we need the signature of the authorities."

Jurek climbed onto the wagon. From the mayor's they continued on their way. Jurek lay in the straw on the bottom of the wagon and fell asleep. He awoke when the farmer stopped his horse. They were in Gestapo headquarters. At first he thought he was having a nightmare. No one had told him that "the authorities" meant the Gestapo. The young officer was standing in the yard. He hurried over to Jurek with a big grin and yanked him out of the wagon.

"So you're back, eh? I know you're a Jew. But this time I'm not going to kill you. You're too smart for that, and I like you."

The astounded farmer let himself be consoled with the bounty he was given for turning in a Jew and drove off. The officer handed Jurek to a soldier. The soldier made him take off his clothes, shaved his head, ordered him to bathe, and gave him clean clothes and a pair of shoes.

"They're the smallest size I have," he said. "Stuff some rags into them."

"Give me back what was in my pockets," Jurek said.

The soldier gave him back his slingshot and Marisza's magnifying glass.

"Where's my knife?"

"The officer kept it."

The soldier took Jurek to a small room with a chair, a table, and a large window looking out on the forest. He had never had his own private room before. Sometimes, at night, screams and moans reached it from the basement, where Jurek had been. He would awake shivering all over. In the morning it was quiet again. A wagon would come and leave with something beneath a tarpaulin.

Jurek became the officer's valet. He cleaned his clothes and brushed his boots. At first, the German wasn't satisfied. He explained that he wanted his boots to be so shiny that he could see his reflection in them. It took Jurek a while to master the art of it. While he was still learning he was given a slap for every speck of dirt on the boots. In his spare time he sat in the kitchen with the Polish cook. He ate so much that he developed a paunch.

"So you're a Jew?" she asked him one day.

"No. I'm not."

"I know you are, son. The officer told me."

Jurek said nothing.

"It's nothing to be ashamed of. Jews are human too."

As though to prove it, she took a large piece of chocolate from the closet and gave it to him.

✡

It was already summer when the officer summoned Jurek one day and said, "Put on your shoes and come with me."

Jurek came back with his shoes on. The officer put him, together with a dog, in the sidecar of his motorcycle, and they set out.

Jurek wondered where he was being taken. Although the German saw the worry in his face, he merely smiled and said nothing. After a while they left the main road and crossed some fields until they came to a big farm.

"The village near here is called Krumnow," the German said, parking in the yard. "I'm bringing you to a girlfriend of mine. You'll work for her. Behave yourself and everything will be all right. And here's your knife back."

"Thank you," Jurek said in German.

The officer dismounted. A young woman came to greet him. She was wearing boots and her sleeves were rolled up to her elbows.

"This is Frau Herman," the officer said, introducing her to Jurek. He winked. "She's the beautiful wife of Meister Herman."

Jurek didn't know why he was being winked at. The officer said to the woman, "I've brought you a new hand. He's an excellent worker. Look how he polishes my boots." He raised one boot for Pani Herman to inspect it.

She looked at Jurek.

"Watch the dog while I'm gone," the officer said. He and Pani Herman walked off, laughing merrily.

Jurek stayed on at Pani Herman's. From her other workers he learned that she was a Pole of German extraction. Her husband worked for the Germans, and she ran their farm by herself. The Gestapo supplied her with free labor from the ranks of convicts and debtors. It didn't take Jurek long to learn that you had to toe the line with her. Any slackers could expect a beating from the Gestapo. He did as he was told and carried out orders promptly and carefully. The work he liked best was taking the cows to pasture, because then he was far away from Pani Herman's demands.

The officer came to visit often. Whenever he saw Jurek, he told him to mind his dog.

"Can I play with it?" Jurek asked him one day in German.

"You know German?"

"A bit."

"I forgot you once had a dog. Yes, you can throw him a stick and tell him to fetch. Say 'Good dog' when he brings it back to you. Can you say that in German?"

Jurek said it.

"Excellent."

Jurek missed Azor.

✡

It was threshing time. The Hermans' farm was large and mechanized. The threshing was done by a machine with huge wooden wheels turned by something called a rotary walker. This was made of cogwheels propelled by a shaft operated by a team of horses driven in a circle. A long, wide belt ran from the shaft to the thresher, from which grains of wheat poured like pure gold.

Jurek was given a whip and told to keep the horses walking steadily. He was proud of his new job and liked to crack his whip from time to time with a sound like a rifle shot, even though it was rarely necessary. For long hours each day he walked behind the horses, who circled on a track of packed dirt. During lunchtime he hung sacks of barley around their necks and joined the other workers for the meal.

On the next-to-last day of threshing, soon after the lunch break, he heard someone shout a warning behind him. There was no time to make sense of it. His whip, trailing behind him, had gotten caught in the cogwheels, dragging his arm into the machine.

"Stop the horses!"

Someone grabbed the horses. Jurek felt an unbearable pain. Someone helped pull his mangled arm from the wheels. He managed to get it into his sleeve before he passed out. From time to time he came to and tried to grasp what was happening. Pani Herman was sitting beside him in a speeding wagon. She tried to keep his arm from being jolted by the bumps. Now and then the blackness that he saw turned to blue and he understood that he was looking at the sky. Then everything was black again.

Jurek was brought to a hospital in Nowy Dwur, a small city on the right bank of the Wisla. He was placed on an examination table and washed by two nurses. Pani Herman went to pay for his hospitalization. When she returned, he was on the operating table. A young surgeon entered. He examined Jurek and said:

"I'm not operating on this boy."

Pani Herman was startled. "Why not?"

"Because he's a Jew."

"He's not a Jew!" she shouted. "I got him from the Gestapo and he's my worker. You'll operate on him at once!"

"He's a Jew," the doctor insisted.

"You don't know what you're talking about!" Pani Herman shouted. "I paid 157 marks and 25 pfennig for him!"

She made a scene, screaming, sobbing, and threatening to call the Gestapo if anything happened to Jurek. Then she drove off.

The doctor refused to back down. He ordered Jurek to be put in the corridor on a stretcher.

Jurek lay there in shock. In the moments when he regained consciousness, he felt as though he and his excruciatingly painful body were two separate things. As soon as they became one again, he passed out. He no longer knew where he was. His lips mumbled words that had no sound.

The next morning the senior surgeon, Dr. Zurawski, arrived. He saw Jurek in the corridor and exclaimed,

"What have you done? You could have saved the boy's arm!"

Jurek was taken to the operating room and anaesthetized. His gangrened arm was amputated above the elbow. When he awoke, he rubbed his eyes and tried lifting it. Nothing moved except for a bandaged stump. He broke into bitter tears. And yet by shutting his eyes he could feel the whole arm again, from his shoulder to his fingertips. He could even feel the whip in his hand.

In the first days after the operation, Jurek cried a lot. The nurses fed him and bathed him. They dressed him in a long hospital gown and he spent hours kneeling by his bed and praying to Jesus and the Virgin Mary. Often, trying to support himself with an arm that wasn't there, he nearly fell. Everything was an overwhelming reminder of his condition.

One morning he was woken by a nun. She bent over him and said, "Come, Jurek, sit up. I'm here to help you."

She took him to the shower and taught him how to wash with his left arm. She showed him how to cross himself and hold a spoon with it.

She came to see him every day.

"There's almost nothing you can't do with one arm," she promised him.

"Are you sure, Sister?"

"Yes. It's only a matter of time and patience."

For the first time since the accident, he felt a spark of hope.

In his second week in the hospital, Jurek began to roam its rooms and corridors. He visited the different wards, was met by smiles, and even began to smile back.

Twice a week someone came with a food package from Pani Herman's farm. The packages were full of good things—hard-boiled eggs, meat, even cake. Now and then Pani Hermann came herself. She never found Jurek in his bed. He had made friends with many of the patients, who knew him and joked with him. One old man taught him to play checkers, and they spent hours at it by his bed. Pani Herman laughed when she saw the two of them.

One day Jurek passed the maternity ward, peered inside, and saw a familiar face. For a moment, he couldn't place it. It belonged to the wife of the couple who had turned him in to the Gestapo. The woman saw him, too. Soon the attitude toward him in the hospital had changed. Patients looked away when he passed. A package disappeared before it reached him.

The old patient went on playing checkers with him.

"Why did they amputate your leg?" Jurek asked him.

"I have diabetes. How about you?"

"I had a bastard for a doctor," Jurek said.

"So I've heard," said the man. "I was told he wouldn't operate because you're a Jew."

"I'm not."

The man didn't argue. He just said, "Jurek, the Gestapo will come for you. You know what they do to Jews. Go to Dr. Zurawski. Talk to him."

Jurek went to the doctor's office.

"Yes, Jurek. How is your arm?"

"The one I don't have? I don't know. The one I have is fine."

The doctor smiled. "What can I do for you?"

"Send me back to the village, Doctor."

110

"I can't."

"Why can't you?"

"I'll tell you the truth. I had a call from the Gestapo. They told me to keep you here until they come for you."

Jurek tried planning an escape. Yet not only did it turn out that there was a guard at the front door, but the nurses had no clothes for him.

"We burned them," he was told. "They were full of lice."

He waited impatiently for the next visit from the village. When a farmhand brought him a package with regards from Pani Herman, he pleaded, "Take me with you."

"Are you allowed to leave?"

"I have to leave."

"I'll ask the doctor," the farmhand said.

"I can't let him go," said Dr. Zurawski. "I have orders from the Gestapo to hold him here."

"Doctor," the man said. "I've heard that Jurek is a Jew. That's hard for me to believe, because we got him from the Gestapo. But if it's true, you know what the Gestapo will do to him."

The doctor frowned. "Medically speaking," he said, "he can go."

"Then I can take him?"

"No. But there's a big window in the bathroom on the floor above us. It faces the back of the building. And I haven't said anything."

Jurek and the farmhand went to the corridor. "Wait beneath the window," Jurek told him.

"But how will you get down?"

"I'll find a way."

Jurek climbed the stairs and entered the bathroom. There was a big window just like the doctor said. He opened it and looked out. The farmhand was below, looking up. Jurek climbed onto the window sill and called down, "Catch me!"

He jumped.

The farmhand caught him. They both fell to the ground. The man rose, picked Jurek up, and ran into the street with him.

Nowy Dwur was on the banks of the Narew River, near where it joined the Wisla. The farmhand carried Jurek to the river and put him in a rowboat. He freed the mooring line and began to row. They headed downstream and moved quickly. It was a whole new experience for Jurek. The farmhand told him to take the rudder.

"Me?"

"It's easy."

He took the rudder.

"I'll say left, right, or straight ahead. Can you tell your left hand from your right?"

The man regretted the question at once. But Jurek just grinned. "Of course I can. It's easy to remember now."

Jurek quickly saw that he could steer with one arm. He sat watching the tugboats and small craft on the river.

"You're bleeding," the farmhand suddenly said in alarm.

The bandages on Jurek's stump were soaked in blood, staining his hospital gown.

"I must have hurt myself when I jumped."

"Does it hurt?"

"No."

"Pani Herman will take care of you, don't worry," the farmhand assured him.

Pani Herman, too, was alarmed by the blood stains. She relaxed only when she changed the bandage and saw it wasn't serious. Instead of sending Jurek back to sleep in the barn, she put him up in a small room in the house.

"You could still mind the cows," she told him the next day. "But when my boyfriend hears that you ran away from the hospital, he'll come looking for you. Now that you only have one arm, I don't know what he'll decide to do with you."

She had her seamstress make Jurek a shirt and a jacket with one short sleeve. The missing sleeve felt like an insult. Then she brought him socks and new shoes.

"I found shoes your size," she told him.

For the first time in his life, Jurek owned a pair of shoes that fit him. Pani Herman made him sit while she laced them. Then she hung a knapsack on his shoulder.

"Don't worry," she said, seeing the concern in his eyes. "Everything you had in the pockets of your old pants is in here. There's a bottle of water, too. Do you need anything else?"

"Yes," Jurek said. "Some rope, matches, and my stick."

Pani Herman sent someone to bring him a length of rope, several boxes of matches, and his walking stick.

"God look after you," she said.

Jurek kissed her hand and left.

12.

With One Hand

Jurek was afraid to go back to the forest. What would he do there? How would he survive? How could he climb a tree or hunt with his slingshot? He could live for a while on berries and mushrooms. But he could also work as a cowherd and earn his keep, if only he could find someone to take a one-armed boy.

As soon as he had put some distance between himself and Pani Herman's farm, he took off his new shoes and put them in his knapsack. He knew he would need them in the winter, if he wasn't caught before then.

The harvested fields were yellow in the early-autumn sun. The forest was green in the distance. Purple heather grew in the untilled fields. Jurek followed a dirt path between them and prayed silently. Not in the words he had learned from the pretty woman. He simply asked God to help him, repeating over and over, O God, O God, O God, O God, O God . . .

Once he had been a Jewish boy. He hadn't forgotten that. Then, too, he had known there was a God. His father and oldest brother had prayed to Him every morning, tying a black box to their foreheads and winding a leather thong around their arms. Although he couldn't remember the words for these things, he could picture the two of them in their white shawls, swaying back and forth in prayer. Sometimes they took him to the synagogue. That was where the Jewish God lived. But now God lived in the churches of little villages and there were three of Him, for he was also Jesus and the Holy Ghost. Jurek touched the cross and the medallion of the Madonna around his neck. How could they have let the young doctor refuse to save his arm?

He came to a low wall ahead by the side of the path. It had a gate with a large metal cross. He went and peered through it. Inside was a cemetery filled with crosses of all kinds and shapes. He opened the gate and entered. Apart from the tombstones, there were several structures that looked like little houses. These were old mausoleums in which nobles and rich landowners had been buried. He approached one of them and tried its low metal door. The door creaked and opened a bit. He pushed again and forced his way inside. He was in a room with two stone benches, one on each side. An old stone coffin lay on one of them. In the middle of the room was a long rectangular pit with a mound of earth. Broken pieces of stone were scattered on it. Jurek tried to open the coffin but couldn't. He went outside and found a shovel without a handle. After many attempts, he managed to pry open the coffin's lid. He feared finding a corpse and hoped to find a treasure. But there was neither. Except for a few bones, the coffin was empty. He threw them in the pit, climbed into the coffin, and lay down. It was comfortable enough for a boy his size.

Jurek decided to made this place his home. He went

outside and found a well at the far end of the cemetery. At least he wouldn't die of thirst here.

The next day he left his knapsack with what remained of the food in the coffin and left the cemetery early. He didn't want to bump into anyone visiting a grave. He spent the day in the forest and came back at night to sleep. When the food was gone, he foraged for vegetables in the nearby villages. Coming across a field of kohlrabi, he bent to dig up a few plants. Suddenly he heard a shout, and a man came running toward him. Turning to flee, he was shocked to see that he had lost partial control of his body and could no longer run and hurdle obstacles as before. The loss of his arm had affected his sense of balance. Though he managed to get away, he spent the next days practicing running and jumping to see how best to do them. Using his slingshot was out of the question. The results with his left hand were so dismal that he soon gave up.

The autumn rains set in. The trees lost their leaves. The berries disappeared from the forest. Seeing the wild boar eat the acorns and horse chestnuts that fell from the trees, he tried roasting these in a fire and eating them, but they weren't edible. Mostly he lived off unharvested vegetables and potatoes left in the gardens. If it was raining and he couldn't light a fire, he ate the potatoes raw.

His favorite occupation was playing with the rope. Using his mouth and feet, he taught himself to tie and untie knots. One day he decided to climb a tree. He heaved one end of the rope over a branch, knotted the two ends, and pulled himself upward. On his first try he slipped and almost fell, grabbing on to a branch at the last second. But after a day of experimenting, he found a system that worked. If he ever had to return to the forest, he would be able to sleep in the trees again.

His success with the rope restored a measure of his self-confidence. If only he dared, he could do many of the things he used to do. It simply took patience, as the nun in the hospital had told him. One day he decided it was time to look for work in the villages.

He opened his knapsack, took the shoes, and put them on. Tying the laces was a problem, because he couldn't raise his foot high enough to grab hold of them with his teeth. But he had an idea. He pulled the lace from the shoe and reinserted it with one end long and the other short. Now he could grip the long end with his teeth, get his foot into the shoe, and knot the short end. He felt proud of this solution. His knapsack on his shoulder, he set out full of hope, tapping with his stick on the tree trunks and running it over the bushes as if they were the picket fences of Blonie.

All at once he found himself facing a big German shepherd dog. Before he knew it he was on the ground and the dog was pinning him, its two front paws on his chest. Panting heavily, it opened a toothy mouth and stuck out a long tongue. Jurek tried to move. The dog growled menacingly. He lay still. A German soldier came up and called off the dog. It obeyed him at once. He hauled Jurek to his feet and said, "So it's you! You're just the person we're looking for."

They walked in silence with Jurek in the middle, flanked by the German and the dog. Although the German did not hold on to him, Jurek knew he had no chance of escaping.

After a while, the soldier began to speak. It wasn't clear if he was talking to Jurek, the dog, or himself.

"If I bring you alive to the Gestapo," he said, "I'll get a commendation for being a good soldier. What good will that do me? And if I kill you and bring you dead to the Gestapo, I'll also get a commendation for being a good soldier. And what good will that do me? What do you think, Rex?"

The dog raised its head and looked at him.

They were near the edge of the forest. The soldier left the path, stepped into the bushes, and bent to lift a rusty iron trapdoor. Descending underground, he told Jurek to follow him. Jurek peered inside. There was an iron ladder, which he climbed down. Below was a bunker with a high window that was too covered with shrubbery to let in much light. There was a bench, a battered chair, and some old army blankets and mattresses along one wall. An open metal cabinet contained a bottle of water and some tins of food. On the shelf above them was a loaf of bread. Obviously, the soldier spent much of his time here.

The German opened a tin, cut a thick slice of bread, spread some meat on it, and handed it to Jurek. He put some meat in a bowl for Rex. The dog just looked at it.

"Good dog," the soldier said. "Eat!"

Rex wolfed down the bowl.

The German took the rest of the meat for himself and sat down on the bench beside Jurek. The three of them ate in silence. When he was finished eating, the German took out a pack of cigarettes.

"Do you smoke?"

A chill ran down Jurek's spine.

"No," he said.

But the soldier didn't look as if he was about to kill him. He took a cigarette lighter from his pocket. Jurek looked at it admiringly.

"Werner," the soldier said, pointing at himself.

"Jurek," said Jurek.

The soldier took out his wallet and showed Jurek a photograph of a woman and two children.

"My wife and kids," he said.

The woman was young and looked nice. The children, a boy and a girl, smiled at Jurek from the photograph. Jurek smiled back.

The soldier laughed. He kissed the photograph and said proudly, "My family! Where is your family?"

Jurek did his best to answer in a German that was more a mixture of Yiddish and Polish:

"We were five. Three boys and two girls. They may all be dead. I saw my father killed in a field. My mother . . . I don't know."

The soldier shook his head sadly.

"War," he said, cursing it. "It's just my luck to have caught a blond, one-armed Jewish boy. What is a blond, one-armed Jewish boy? He's only a boy. And what am I? I'm only a soldier. Isn't that so, Rex?"

The dog raised its head. Werner went on talking. Jurek didn't understand very much. Here and there he made out a word. God. People. What will be the end?

Before leaving, the soldier told him he could use the bunker all he wanted. "Just close the door when you leave. I'll be back."

A few days later he came back with more tins. He

didn't come at regular intervals. Sometimes he slept there. Conversation was difficult. Jurek's German wasn't good enough and Werner knew even less Polish. He made up for it by slapping Jurek on the shoulder or patting him on the head and giving him candy or chocolate. Jurek looked forward to each visit. In between, he missed the soldier more and more. It was hard to say goodbye. He knew that was coming when Werner started looking at his watch.

He had an idea. Taking a crate, he drew a checkerboard on it with the help of some charred wood he had found. Then he collected twenty-four acorns, blackened half of them, and waited. Eventually, Werner and Rex appeared. The dog ran happily to Jurek. Werner put some new tins of food in the closet and placed a loaf of bread on the bench. Then he caught sight of the surprise. He grinned broadly and patted Jurek's head. After eating they sat down to a game of checkers.

Werner always had time for at least three games. Whenever Jurek beat him, he was as happy as Jurek.

One day Jurek came back from the forest and found a loaf of bread and two new tins of food. Werner's lighter was lying on one of them. He felt heartbroken. He knew he would never see the German soldier again.

✡

Jurek remained in the bunker until he finished the food. Then he went to look for farm work.

In the first village he came to, a gang of boys sicced their dog on him. He tried to run but the dog was too fast. He turned and struck it on the snout with his stick, the way he once saw Avrum do. The dog yowled and ran off. But the boys continued to hector him and throw stones until he was out of the village.

A long walk brought him to the next village. It looked familiar. Taken aback, he stopped to regard the houses. Suddenly he heard shouts. A group of German soldiers had noticed him and was running in his direction. But now he knew where he was. Without hesitating, he ran to the pretty woman's house and knocked. She opened the door, took one look at him, and sank to the floor with a groan.

"Hide me, ma'am!" he cried. "They're after me."

The woman pulled herself together. She led Jurek inside and opened a trapdoor in the kitchen. He climbed into the cellar and she shut the door and poured water on the floor to wash away his footprints.

The Germans burst inside and began to search.

"Who are you looking for?" she asked.

"The one-armed Jewish boy."

"I haven't seen any boy."

"We saw him run in here."

"No one is here," the woman insisted.

The soldiers combed the house, sticking their bayonets wherever a child might have been hiding. They seemed to take pleasure in the damage they did. One bayoneted a straw basket in which a hen was sitting on her eggs.

"Are you going to hand him over or not?" they asked.

"There's no one here," the woman repeated.

The Germans were furious. They beat her, dragged her out of the house, and set it on fire. Then they torched the whole village.

Jurek sat huddled in darkness. He heard the woman's screams, the Germans' curses, and the heavy steps of boots. Screams came from everywhere. The cellar filled with smoke. He heard heavy objects tumbling to the floor above him. He didn't know they were the rafters of the house. It was hard to breathe. He was gasping for air. After what might have been long hours or only a few minutes, the trapdoor opened and he saw light.

"You can come out," said the woman. "Jurek? Are you all right? You can come out. They're gone."

He climbed out of the cellar. He hardly recognized her. She was not the same woman who had opened the door for him a short while before. She was old and beaten, and her clothes were torn. He looked in horror at the ruined, half-burned house.

"Is this because of me?" he asked, racked by spasms of coughing.

She didn't answer. She took him outside, scooped some water from a puddle, and washed his face with it. Then she washed her own face. He looked around. The village was no longer there. The houses stood charred and smoking. Some were still burning. People stood helplessly in the street. Farmers carried water from the well and threw it on the smoldering ruins. Women wailed.

He pointed to the smoking village with horror. "Is this because of me?" he asked again.

"No. It's not because of you. You may have been the reason they burned my house first. But they've been here for the past three days. They know we helped the partisans. They beat us, they shot us, and today they burned our village. What happened to your arm?"

"It was caught in a machine."

"Jurek, I can't help you anymore. You have to go now. And don't come back. I've had all I can take. Do you understand? I can't take any more of this. I don't even have food to give you. Just keep walking east. Do you know where east is? It's where the sun rises in the morning. That's where the Russians will come from. Dear Jesus, save this boy from harm."

She crossed herself. Big tears ran down her cheeks.

Who were the Russians? He didn't ask.

13.

An Unknown Soldier

He walked toward the east, keeping close to the villages by the edge of the forest. He never entered them during the day. He was known and on the Wanted list. His third day on the road gave him additional proof of this. As he was thinking of how old, stooped, and crushed the pretty woman had become in a few minutes, he saw two Germans on horseback coming toward him. He recognized them at once. They were the soldiers who had chased him after he escaped from Gestapo headquarters. He pulled his hat over his eyes and kept walking while turning his right side away from them. It seemed to work. They passed him and rode on. Each time he turned around to look, they were smaller against the background of the cloudy sky. Yet suddenly they stopped, wheeled, and galloped toward him. He left the road and sprinted toward the forest. As he reached the tree line, a horse-drawn wagon piled with firewood came toward him. Driving it was Werner. Jurek ran to him with relief and cried, "Quick, hide me! They're after me!"

But up close he saw it wasn't Werner at all. It was an unknown soldier. The hat and uniform were the same, but not the face. For a second, Jurek froze. Before he could get a grip on himself, the soldier grabbed him by the collar, hoisted him into the wagon, pushed him under the seat, and sat down on it.

The two mounted soldiers galloped up. Only now did the driver of the wagon realize who Jurek was hiding from. Their Gestapo uniforms were easily recognizable.

"Have you seen a blond, one-armed Jewish boy?" they asked.

"Yes," the soldier said, pointing to the forest. "He went that way."

Jurek heard the horses gallop off. The wagon lurched slowly out of the forest and onto the paved road. The driver whistled. After a while he asked in broken Polish:

"Where to?"

"Where are you going?" Jurek asked from under the seat.

The soldier laughed. "To Nowy Dwur."

"That's good enough for me," Jurek said. He thought for a minute and asked, "Is that across the Wisla?"

"Yes."

"That's very good." This time Jurek spoke German.

"You know German?"

"A bit."

The soldier stopped the wagon, cleared some room amid the firewood, and moved Jurek to it from his place beneath the seat.

"Lie down here," he said.

He took off his coat and covered him. "Now no one will see you."

He whipped the horses.

"Are you really a Jew?"

"No," Jurek said.

"Tell the truth."

"No. I'm not."

"What's your name?"

"Jurek Staniak."

"I mean your real name."

Jurek paused to reflect. He couldn't remember it.

"I've forgotten," he said.

The soldier resumed whistling. After a while he asked, "Are you hungry?"

"Yes."

He took a large sandwich from a box by his feet and gave it to Jurek. When Jurek had finished eating and lain down again, the soldier asked what happened to his arm.

Jurek told him.

"Where will you go in Nowy Dwur?"

"I'm not going anywhere in Nowy Dwur. I'll get off before that. As soon as we cross the Wisla."

"Why do you want to cross the Wisla?"

"Because everyone around here knows me."

"The one-armed Jewish boy?"

"Yes," Jurek said.

The traffic on the road grew heavier. Farm wagons passed in both directions. German army trucks went by. There were military motorcycles with sidecars and an occasional soldier or Polish worker on a bicycle. They reached the bridge over the Wisla and crossed it. The rattle of the wheels on the wooden bridge made Jurek sit up to look.

"Lie down," the German said sternly.

On the other side of the bridge, he stopped the horses

and helped Jurek to get out. He reached into his box and gave him another sandwich. "For the road," he said.

"Thank you very much," Jurek told him.

"God look after you, boy."

The soldier climbed back on the wagon and drove off. Jurek walked quickly away from the road and found a dirt path that wound between fields and meadows. He gazed at the horizon. Here and there were what looked like small woods, but nowhere did he see the reassuring black line of a large forest. The small town of Nowy Dwor was at his back. He walked on, trying to put his painful memories behind him.

It began to rain. Not until evening did he spy the smoke of chimneys spiraling up to the low, cloudy black sky. He tramped through mud until he reached the village. Its thatched roofs were blurry in the fog. He came to a farm. Going to the door of the farmhouse, he knocked. A farmer opened, regarded him hesitantly, and let him into the house. Two young girls and a middle-aged woman were sewing by the stove. Jurek politely doffed his cap and greeted them.

The women greeted him back.

"Help him out of his jacket," the woman said. "Sit the boy at the table."

The farmer helped Jurek out of his jacket and hung it by the stove to dry. One of the girls filled a plate from a bowl on the table and gave it to Jurek. On it were potatoes with sour cream, cooked carrots, and an omelet with large slices of sausage. Jurek didn't look up until he was finished eating.

The questions began. He was used to them. He told

them his name and his story. Then he laid his head on the table and shut his eyes.

"The boy is tired," the woman said.

"Come," said the farmer. "I'll put you to bed."

His wife gave him a nightshirt and two blankets. He took a lantern and ran through the rain with Jurek to the hayloft. Jurek heard a loud banging, as if someone were firing bullets at the roof.

"What's that?" he asked in a fright.

"What's what?" The farmer didn't know what he meant.

"That noise . . ."

The farmer laughed.

"It's the rain on the tin roof," he said.

"How can anyone sleep with that noise?" Jurek asked.

"You'll get used to it. You can't sleep in the hayrack in the barn because there are bags of seed in it."

The farmer waited for Jurek to make his bed and returned to the house. Jurek was left alone in the dark. He took off his wet clothes, put on the nightshirt, and lay down beneath the blankets. Yet he couldn't fall asleep. He had never heard rain drumming on a tin roof before. Although in the end his fatigue got the best of him, he kept waking from time to time, the sound of the rain drifting in and out of his dreams. One dream was an old one. In it he was climbing a tree. Suddenly he slipped and reached out to grab a branch. But the hand he reached with belonged to his missing arm and he fell. The falling woke him. He clutched at the hay beneath him and let out a horrible moan. He opened his eyes. But it wasn't he who had moaned. The moans were coming from the darkness.

Two beams of light were moving toward him.

"Aaaooowwww . . . Aaaooowwww . . ."

Jurek jumped up and ran for dear life. He crossed the yard and burst into the farmhouse. The last embers in the stove threw some light on the floor. He sat shaking with fear. The creak of the door woke the farmer, who stepped out of the bedroom. Seeing the apparition in white by the stove, he crossed himself fearfully and exclaimed, "Mama! What are you doing here?"

Several days previously, it seemed, the farmer's mother had died. Now he was sure he was looking at her ghost.

"It's just me," Jurek said. "Jurek Staniak."

The farmer grabbed him, hit him, and threw him from the house. "Go to sleep!" he yelled.

Jurek returned reluctantly to the hayloft. He was wide awake. Groping his way to his bed of straw, he found his pants, took Werner's lighter from a pocket, and lit it. Two cats were lying on his blanket. He crept under it with both of them, repeating out loud in as deep a voice as he could muster, "Mama! What are you doing here?"

He burst into laughter.

The next morning, seeing the farmer and his younger daughter near a wheelbarrow of mash for the pigs, he went up and asked for work.

"How can you work with one arm?" the farmer asked.

"I can do anything. Whatever you need done."

"Can you push this wheelbarrow to the pigsty?" the farmer asked.

"Sure," Jurek said. "I'll show you."

He took his rope, doubled it, measured off the distance from his right shoulder to the handle of the wheelbarrow, made a sheepshank with the help of his feet, and looped one end of the rope around the handle and the other over the shoulder. He now had a second arm. The farmer and his daughter watched curiously. Jurek seized the other handle with his good arm and straightened up. Although he had never done it before, he managed to keep the wheelbarrow on an even keel while pushing it safely over the planks to the pigsty.

"Papa, let's take him," the girl said.

"No," the farmer replied. "What you just did was impressive, but I need someone with two hands."

"I'll help him," said the girl.

"You'd better remember you said that, Marina," her father told her.

He turned to Jurek.

"Take that bucket and fill the trough."

14.

Marina and Grzegorz

Stanislaw Boguta didn't give Jurek special consideration for being without an arm. He treated him like any boy given food and board for his labor. He assigned him every kind of chore and hit him when he did something wrong. Without intending to, he helped Jurek in his struggle to be normal.

When Jurek kept complaining about the sound of the rain on the roof, Marina and her mother cleared part of the hayrack in the barn for him. Reached by rungs on the wall, it was high enough above the floor to keep the cows from getting at it. The warmth they gave off was a natural heating system. Jurek took the two cats from the hayloft, and they continued to sleep with him.

He soon realized that Marina was her mother's favorite. Clara, the oldest daughter, was closer to her father. Perhaps this was why all eyes were on Pani Boguta when she served the meat at Sunday dinner. Yet try as she might to give everyone the same size portion, Clara would angrily declare, "You've gone and given Marina the best part again!"

Marina would switch her plate with Clara's, and Clara would angrily snatch her plate back again.

Stanislaw Boguta was bored by the winter days, on which there was little to do. Tired of making the rounds of the house and yard to find something for his daughters and Jurek to do, he would harness the horse to a sled if the farm was not snowed in and drive into town to sit with his friends in the tavern.

This left Clara in charge. She never allowed Jurek to go play with the village boys before he had finished all his chores—feeding the pigs and chickens, collecting the eggs, giving the cows and horses fresh hay—and would invent new tasks if she thought he had finished too soon.

"Go chop some wood, Jurek," she might say.

Although he could chop wood with one arm, it took him a long time.

"Aren't you done yet?" she would ask.

"Leave him alone," Marina would say, coming to his defense.

"Now sort potatoes."

Jurek went to the storeroom to sort potatoes. Clara came, took a look, and berated him for a careless job. He sorted them again and tried slipping away when he was done, but she was waiting for him outside.

"Go fetch some firewood!"

Not having two arms for the wood, he tied it with a rope and carried it on his back. One day a poorly tied knot came apart and the wood fell in the snow. Marina hurried out to help Jurek pick it up and bring it into the house. Then, while Clara watched disapprovingly, she told him he was free.

"Clara hates everyone because she's not married," she said to him with a giggle.

Marina was as good as her word. One morning the wheelbarrow turned over as Jurek was pushing it to the pigsty along the icy planks. Pan Boguta cuffed him as usual. From then on, every morning and evening, Marina fed the pigs. If not for her, Jurek would have had to go elsewhere despite the snow and the cold.

The village children liked to build snowmen with coals for eyes and a carrot for a nose. Jurek rarely joined them, because it was a morning game and he was busy. Snowball fights, though, went on throughout the short winter days. There was also a hill at the end of the village, down which the children sledded with merry whoops. Some used boards and others had homemade sleds. Despite his handicap, Jurek was athletic; well-liked because of his good nature, he was welcome in all the children's games. If he couldn't get away from Clara's sharp eyes before dark, he'd sit by the stove with the women, watching them sew, launder, or iron until it was time to go to sleep in the barn.

One Sunday a young man came riding up and tied his horse to the fence. Marina, looking out the window, saw him enter the yard. "Grzegorz!" she shouted, running to him happily.

Pan Boguta followed her outside, grabbed her by the arm, and dragged her back into the house. He gave the young man an unfriendly look and said, "You can come court Clara, if you want. Marina is too young."

When the youngster was gone he said to Marina, "He's just a carpenter. He has no land and he isn't from these parts. I don't want you going out with him. If I catch you with him, I'll lock you in the house. I wouldn't want to be in his shoes when I get hold of him."

"But why can he court Clara?" Marina asked.

"If Clara would like him to, I have no objection," her father said. "Better a carpenter's wife than an old maid."

Clara burst into bitter tears. It was the first and last time that Jurek ever felt sorry for her.

Jurek knew Grzegorz. He was the young man who said hello to Marina every Sunday in church. Jurek saw the passionate glances they exchanged during the service. One day Marina asked Jurek to lag behind the next time they came out of church.

"Grzegorz will give you a note," she said. "When nobody is looking, you'll pass it to me. Can you read?"

"No."

Marina was happy to hear that. From then on Grzegorz handed a note to Jurek every Sunday, and Jurek passed it to Marina. Before the winter was over, Grzegorz began coming to the farm at night. Sunday night was his usual time. Marina would slip out of the house and wait for him in the barn. Since she had no one else to talk to it about, she bared her heart to Jurek.

"He's awfully good-looking, isn't he?"

Jurek didn't know if Grzegorz was good-looking or not, but he agreed anyway.

"I once saw a closet he made for the parents of a friend of mine," Marina went on. "And a coffin he made for our neighbor. He's an artist. I tell you, Jurek, he has hands of gold. And a brain, too! I love him. I don't care what my father says. He can do what he wants. I'll elope and marry him. It's all Clara's fault."

It would be sad if Marina left, Jurek thought.

Each time Grzegorz came, they stood embracing each

other in the darkness by the cows. Eventually, Jurek fell asleep. When he awoke again, they were still locked in an embrace.

"Aren't you cold?" he once asked Marina.

"No," she said. "Love warms you, even in the winter."

One night they asked Jurek to sleep in the hayloft.

"We'll wake you later and you'll come back to the barn," they said.

Although Jurek would have slept anywhere for Marina's sake, he was curious. What could they be doing there in the hayrack, under his blankets?

One night his curiosity got the better of him. Quietly, he sneaked back into the barn and hid among the cows. It was too dark to see. But he heard Marina and Grzegorz whispering and making noises. While he wasn't sure what they were doing, he was excited in a strange new way. He went back to the hayloft and lay there thinking. He could remember sleeping with his mother and being woken and told in the middle of the night, "Srulik, move to your father's bed."

Half-conscious, he had changed beds and fallen asleep at once.

He was thinking so hard now that he sat up. He recalled a conversation between his big brothers. One of them said, "Papa tossed Mama his hat tonight and she didn't toss it back."

They laughed, then noticed him listening curiously.

"Srulik, do you know what happens when Mama keeps Papa's hat?"

"He wears another one," Srulik said.

They laughed harder. Now, in the hayloft, Jurek realized

something was eluding him. He racked his brain to understand what it was. Was it the same thing Marisza had
meant when she said, "You'll understand when you're
older"? He didn't want to wait that long. A thought
crossed his mind. No, he told himself. No, it can't be.
Then he fell asleep and didn't awake until Grzegorz came
to take him back to the barn.

One moonlit winter night, after Grzegorz had returned
him to the hayloft, Jurek waited a while and crept back to
the barn. The moonlight glittered on the snow and all was
bright. He hid among the cows. Grzegorz and Marina lay
beneath the blankets. Their clothes hung on the ladder
rungs. He heard footsteps crunching through the snow.
Peering out, he saw Clara. He ran to the hayrack and
whispered:

"Marina, don't move. Clara's here."

He crawled under the blanket with the two of them.

"Jurek?" Clara called from the doorway.

"What?"

"Aren't you asleep?"

"You just woke me."

"Have you seen Marina?"

"No."

"Whose horse is tied to the gate?"

Grzegorz had been careless. You could get away with
things like that on a dark winter night, but not on a night
like this.

Clara came closer to the hayrack.

"What's hanging there?"

"My pants," Jurek said.

"Since when do you sleep without pants?"

She climbed up to look, jumped down, and ran toward the house screaming, "Papa! Marina and Grzegorz are in the barn! Papa!"

The yellow light of a candle appeared in a window. A barefoot Pan Boguta ran outside in his nightshirt, holding a lantern in one hand and an ax in the other. Grzegorz fled. Marina put on her nightdress and shoes and wrapped herself in her sheepskin coat. Her father grabbed her by the hair and dragged her into the house. She didn't cry. There were shouts. Jurek hoped Marina's father wouldn't beat her. He didn't care if Clara never married in her life. He hated her.

In the morning, Pan Boguta threw Jurek out. It was as if he were to blame. Marina came to say goodbye. She kissed him and whispered, "Go to Grzegorz."

Jurek went to the carpentry shop and received a friendly welcome. He was put to work with two young assistants. Although at first they made fun of him, they soon saw that he worked well and seriously. He learned to do things that didn't call for two hands, such as planing, sanding, priming wood, and sawing it in a vise. He was especially good at varnishing furniture. Grzegorz was pleased with him. When he played with the village children after work, he was treated with respect. For the first time in many months he slept in a warm, heated house.

✡

That spring, Grzegorz sold his horse and wagon and packed his things in two large trunks. The farmer who bought the wagon brought him and Jurek to the train station.

"Have you ever ridden in a train?" Grzegorz asked him.

"No," Jurek said, his eyes bright with excitement.

When the train pulled in, Grzegorz was excited too. He kept looking at the windows of the cars, as if searching for someone.

"There she is!" Jurek shouted, catching sight of Marina.

They put the trunks in the baggage car and boarded the train. Marina gave Grzegorz an emotional hug. Tears were running down her cheeks. She kissed Jurek.

"Where are you coming from?" he asked her.

"I was hiding at my aunt's in town. My father came looking for me." She laughed. "You should have seen him, Grzegorz."

"But how did you arrange to meet here?"

"We wrote each other letters. Now you see why you should learn to read and write."

At one of the stations, there was a sudden rush to the windows. German soldiers were standing on the platform. They didn't look about to board the train. A commotion broke out. The younger passengers jumped into the field on the train's other side and began to run. But soldiers were waiting for them there, too. Shots were fired.

"They're rounding up work gangs," Grzegorz said in alarm. "Come on!"

Grzegorz and Marina jumped from the car. Jurek ran to the window. He didn't see them among the passengers climbing over the embankment and running into the field. Nor were they in the ditch at the foot of the embankment or next to the two ruined buildings nearby. He looked back at the field. The frantically running people were further away. The soldiers were firing. Someone fell. Then someone else.

Two soldiers with loaded guns came aboard and grabbed a few young men who had remained on the train. The locomotive whistled. Jurek took his knapsack and got off. No one paid him any attention. Over a dozen young men were standing under guard. The Germans marched them to an army truck waiting outside the station. The train whistled again. Jurek stood on the steps of the car. Marina and Grzegorz were nowhere in sight. The stationmaster and the conductor went from car to car, shutting the doors.

"Are you boarding, son?"

"I'm looking for my brother and sister," Jurek said.

"Those bastards need workers for their fortifications," the conductor declared. "The Russians are coming." He shut the door with a bang.

The train whistled one last time and began to move. Jurek trotted alongside it, hoping to spot Marina and Grzegorz at the last moment and hop aboard. The train picked up speed and he stopped at the end of the platform. And just then he saw them, in a little compartment at the back of the baggage car. They saw him at the same moment. The train went faster. Grzegorz opened the window and shouted. Jurek couldn't make out the words.

15.

Mines

Jurek resumed his wandering life. Sometimes he found work with a farmer for a week or two. Sometimes he stole into a hayloft and spent the night there. In hot weather he looked for streams or lakes to bathe in.

He missed the forest, with its berries and mushrooms. Sometimes he found blueberries and wild strawberries in the woods he passed, but the local women and children had usually beaten him to them. There were vegetables in the fields and in the gardens by the houses. Now and then he was caught, most often while trying to steal chickens. At such times, having only one arm protected him. He was a poor orphan who had to cross himself left-handed, and the farmers didn't beat him.

When he met workers in the fields, he greeted them in the name of Jesus. If he received a friendly greeting in return, he pitched in to help. During breaks he was given food and asked questions. The farmers shook their heads at his sad fate. He didn't like being felt sorry for. They had seen that he could work as well as anyone. He could earn his keep with just one arm.

"Where are you from, son?"

"I don't remember."

Sometimes these encounters ended with a job. One farmer, who ran into him one morning as he was walking sleepily out of a hayloft, offered him a job as a shepherd.

One evening it rained cats and dogs. Jurek was soaked to the bone. The farmer felt bad for him and brought him into the house, where he gave him supper and made a bed for him by the stove. Jurek lay down and was covered with a sheepskin. In the morning the farmer's wife came to wake him. She lifted the sheepskin and let out a scream. "Heniek!" she cried to her husband. "Look! The boy's lice are all over the sheepskin."

The farmer came in, looked at the sheepskin, gave Jurek a slap, and threw him out of the house. He hung the sheepskin on a fence, brought Jurek a comb, and told him to comb out the lice. Jurek put down the comb and took to the road, leaving his lice behind.

Another farmer sent him to the river with his horse. "Take Kasztan and wash him," he said. "Can you do it with one hand?"

"Of course," Jurek said.

When he returned he asked, "Why is the Wisla so little here?"

The farmer laughed and explained that the river wasn't the Wisla. It was another river, the Liwiec, which flowed into the Bug.

Jurek pastured the man's cows for several days. He liked the farm and its family liked him, and he looked forward to remaining. Unexpectedly, however, some cousins soon arrived with two teenage boys and Jurek wasn't needed anymore. The cousins had come from the east, where the Russians were advancing. By now Jurek knew that the thunder and lightning that he had heard and seen at night were the sounds and flashes of the Russians' big guns.

✡

For the second straight day, he was following a broad road. It was strange that, although he could tell it had once been a paved highway, no one was traveling on it. For a while it followed the banks of a river. Jurek decided to bathe in it. He took off his clothes and waded into the water. Nearby was a bridge. He heard the motor of an approaching car and hid. A German truck with several soldiers pulled up on the bridge and stopped. Jurek was frightened. Were they going to swim in the river? He took his clothes and crouched in the reeds. No one entered the water. He peeked out. The men were still on the bridge. He crawled forward for a better look. They were unloading equipment from the truck and doing something on and underneath the bridge.

He wanted to get away. Yet even though he had never heard the word "mines," something told him that the soldiers were planting them. He took some carrots from his knapsack and chewed on them while the Germans worked quickly. Now and then, one took out binoculars and scanned the horizon. They looked worried and left in a hurry.

Jurek made up his mind to remain and warn anyone using the bridge. He found a comfortable place by the riverbank and dozed off. No one came. The sun was setting. He had to look for something to eat. Stepping out of the reeds, he saw a slowly moving wagon.

He flagged down the driver. The man reined in his horses.

"Looking for a ride, boy?"

"Some Germans were here and did something to the bridge. They worked on it a long time."

"Mines!" the man exclaimed. "Son, you may have saved my life. Come, I'll take you home. Are you from that village?" He pointed to his rear.

"Yes," Jurek said. He was about to climb onto the wagon when the farmer stopped him and said:

"Listen, son. The Russians are coming. We heard their artillery all night. They have to be warned that the Germans have mined the bridge. Stay here and keep anyone from crossing. Don't cross yourself. Just yell 'Mines!' if anyone comes near. I'll round up some men in the village and return. And then I'll take you home."

"But I'm hungry," Jurek said.

"I'll give you something to eat."

The farmer pulled a quarter of a loaf of bread and some pears from beneath the driver's seat. He rummaged through his pockets and gave Jurek some sugar cubes. Then he thought for a moment, reached into another pocket, and produced a piece of sausage.

"You deserve it," he said.

Evening arrived and no one came. Jurek sat in a field near the bridge. He tried to stay awake. What would happen when the Russians came? What language would they speak? Russian, he supposed.

That night there were more thunderclaps and light flashes, stronger and closer than before.

In the morning he awoke with a start. Something was making a lot of noise. In the dawn light he saw a row of tanks standing by some army trucks by the bridge, their motors running. Soldiers were standing nearby. He had to warn them about the bridge! He jumped to his feet and ran toward it as fast as he could. A soldier with sergeant's stripes grabbed him and swung him in the air. The soldier smiled and said in Russian, "We're Russian soldiers. Don't be afraid, boy."

Jurek understood him. Russian was like Polish. He tried explaining about the bridge, talking excitedly. The Russian sergeant put him down and said something, but this time he didn't know what it meant. The sergeant was young and broad-shouldered and had a smile that inspired trust. When Jurek kept talking urgently, he took him to a vehicle painted with a red cross.

"He speaks Polish," he said, pointing to a soldier in the vehicle with the same red cross on his sleeve and cap.

"What is it?" the medic asked Jurek.

"The Germans mined the bridge."

"How do you know?"

"I saw them. Yesterday. I was bathing in the river. A farmer told me to stay and warn people while he went to get men from the village. But he never came back."

"We were warned," the medic said. "The villagers told us. That's why we've stopped on this side of the river. We're waiting for the mines to be cleared."

"I fell asleep," Jurek said.

"They told us a boy saw the Germans mine the bridge. Was that you?"

"Yes," Jurek said.

The medic translated the conversation for the sergeant. The sergeant spoke to Jurek warmly. Although Jurek failed to understand the words, he could feel the intention behind them.

"You've saved many lives, son," the medic said. "We'll take you home and give your parents a reward. Where do you live?"

Jurek drew a circle with his one arm. "Everywhere."

"Don't you have a family?"

"No."

"What are you doing around here?"

"I was looking for work."

"What happened to your arm?"

"Are you a doctor?" Jurek asked.

"No," the man said. "I'm a medic."

"It was caught in a machine."

The two men exchanged a few sentences. The medic turned to Jurek. "The sergeant here is asking if you'd like to stick with him," he said. "I'd adopt you myself, because I speak Polish, but I'm leaving for Moscow soon. I won't rejoin the unit until next winter."

Jurek looked at the broad-shouldered sergeant. The sergeant pointed to himself and said, "Sasha."

Jurek did the same thing and said, "Jurek."

Sasha stuck out his hand and they shook.

"Tell him I'll stick with him," Jurek told the medic.

"That's a wise decision," the medic said. "Sasha is a good fellow."

The medic took out some bread and a round box full of silver triangles. He cut a slice of bread, peeled silver foil from a triangle, smeared something yellow on the bread, and handed it to Jurek.

"Do you know what this is?" he asked.

"No."

"Cheese that came all the way from America."

"It did?"

"Yes. So did those trucks and the cans of Spam that you'll eat until you're sick of it. It's all from America."

Jurek knew America was far away. He asked how the trucks had come from there.

"By ship, son," the medic said. "Across the North Sea."

Sasha returned with a uniform. He borrowed scissors from the medic and shortened the sleeves and pants. Then he pointed to the river to tell Jurek to bathe before putting it on.

Word of the one-armed boy and the mined bridge went around among the soldiers. They all were friendly. Jurek spent the day hanging around the tanks and admiring them. When it was time for the soldiers to wash and lubricate them, he grabbed a rag and joined the work. That evening they sat around a campfire. A large pot of kasha was hung above the fire to cook. When it was ready, tins of American Spam were opened and added to it. Sasha gave Jurek a spoon and they ate from the same tin cup. He talked and joked in Russian as though Jurek understood. When the soldiers drifted away from the fire, he took Jurek to a truck, lit a flashlight, and shone it inside the truck. It was filled with tools and instruments. It made Jurek think of the blacksmith's shop in Blonie. Sasha pointed to the tools, then to a tank, and thumped his chest. Jurek understood. Sasha was a tank mechanic. He spread a blanket by the truck and invited Jurek to lie down next to him.

The next morning the unit moved out. Jurek sat with Sasha and a few other soldiers on one of the tanks. At first, despite his protests, Sasha held on to him. After a while, though, he learned to respect Jurek's independence, even though he had only one arm.

Suddenly there was a burst of gunfire. The tank crew jumped into the tank and the other soldiers hit the ground. The tank swiveled its turret, looking for the Germans who had started shooting. There was a firefight. The soldiers on the ground fixed bayonets and charged behind their officer. Jurek, worried about Sasha, raised himself to see what was happening. There was too much dust and smoke to see.

After a while the shooting stopped. He heard cheers. Some soldiers came back pushing three frightened German prisoners ahead of them. Suddenly one of the soldiers let loose a long volley. The Germans fell to the ground in a pool of blood. Jurek fought back his nausea and went to look at the dead men. No, Werner was not one of them. He turned away and saw Sasha.

Sasha looked at him.

"You're pale, Jurek. Get away from there."

Sasha and his crew of mechanics took some tools from the truck and set to work on a tank. Jurek watched them. Sasha pointed to a tool. Jurek handed it to him. Then he handed him another one. Sasha taught him the names of the tools in Russian.

The men stopped for a cigarette break. Jurek took his lighter and lit Sasha's cigarette. Everyone wanted to see it. It passed from hand to hand.

✡

The unit advanced, sometimes fighting and sometimes waiting. Jurek's friendship with Sasha grew stronger. At first they couldn't communicate. Sometimes, though, the Russian and Polish words for things were similar. That made them burst into happy laughter.

"Would you like to eat something different for a change?" Sasha asked one night after their usual meal of kasha and Spam.

Jurek laughed. Sasha's Russian sounded as if he were trying to speak bad Polish to be funny.

"Yes," he said.

"Tomorrow morning."

That night they bivouacked by a lake. The next morning Sasha took a crate and a hand grenade and went to the lakeshore with Yurek. He pulled the pin from the grenade and tossed it into the water. A few seconds later there was an explosion and waves. After a while the bodies of dead fish began to surface, bellies up. Sasha undressed and swam out to gather them. They filled the crate with the fish and brought them back. The soldiers were delighted. The unit had to move out before the fish could be cooked, but they grilled and ate them at their next rest stop.

Despite their language problem, Sasha managed to tell Jurek about his family. Using his hands, he explained that he had an elder brother in the army, two younger sisters, and a little brother smaller than Jurek. Jurek told Sasha about his own family. He was also one of five children, but the youngest. Then Sasha told Jurek the names of his parents, brothers, and sisters. Jurek wanted to do the same, but he couldn't remember anyone's name.

"I forget," he said sadly.

"Where are they?"

Jurek shrugged. "Maybe dead," he said after a while.

Sasha consoled him with a warm slap on the shoulder.

The boom and flash of artillery shells grew further away as the front receded. One day their unit was ordered to halt while the rest of the army continued to advance. Jurek asked the medic why. The medic was sitting on the ground, playing checkers with his driver.

"The army is moving on to the Wisla, son. It will dig in there."

"What about us?"

"We're in luck. We're being saved for the big push on Berlin. Meanwhile we're in summer camp."

Jurek stayed to watch the game. When it was over, he challenged the medic to another.

"You want to play me?" The medic laughed. "All right."

Jurek lost. They played again and he lost again.

"Never mind," the medic consoled him. "Come and play some more. You learn by losing."

He came back often and lost each time. But he didn't give up. The medic was right. His checkers game was improving.

✡

"Sasha, would you like to eat something different?"

It had turned into a game. Jurek was hiding something behind his back.

"Yes," Sasha said.

Jurek opened his hand. There was a slug in it. Sasha burst out laughing. He pushed Jurek to the ground and pretended to make him eat the gooey snail without a shell.

The next day he got back by asking, "Jurek, would you like to eat something different?"

Jurek didn't know what to answer. Perhaps Sasha had some American cheese for him. He took a chance and said "yes." Sasha opened a hand. It held an earthworm. He opened the second and gave Jurek two cubes of sugar.

"Jurek, would you like to eat something different?"

"Yes."

Sasha held out his hands. They were empty.

"Come with me to the village," he said, pointing at some nearby houses.

Jurek conducted the negotiations. He struck a deal to swap sugar for a chicken. He and Sasha walked happily back to their camp and invited the medic to join them for some baked mud chicken.

"How about a game of checkers?" the medic said to Jurek when they had eaten.

Jurek won.

It was his first victory. His joy knew no bounds. The medic rose, handed him the checkerboard and the pieces, and said they were his.

"Take it and teach Sasha how to play," he said. "I'm leaving tomorrow."

He shook Jurek's hand warmly.

Jurek stayed with Sasha and his crew through the autumn and into the winter. By then he could speak enough Russian to be the unit's interpreter. Sasha took him along to the villages to barter.

When the ground frosted over, their unit moved to a village. Sasha's crew was billeted in a big hayloft that belonged to the Cherka family. After a while Sasha began to bring Pani Cherka gifts of food. She accepted them suspiciously. She knew that all the soldiers had their eyes on her daughter Christina, whom she guarded like a watchdog. One day Sasha asked Jurek to write Christina a note in Polish.

Jurek was upset. He feared he was about to lose Sasha just as he had lost Grzegorz and Marina.

"I can't write," he said.

"Fine. Then go talk to her when she's alone in the sheep pen or the barn. Tell her . . ." Sasha hesitated. He wasn't sure how to put it. "Tell her that Sasha says she's beautiful. And when she asks, who's Sasha, you'll point me out. I'll be standing in front of the hayloft, all right?"

"All right."

He carried out his mission successfully. The braided girl really asked, "Who's Sasha?"

"I'll show him to you."

Sasha was standing in front of the hayloft.

"That's him," Jurek said.

Sasha grinned and took a bow. Christina blushed and ran back to the barn.

"Good boy," Sasha said, patting Jurek's shoulder. "Would you like to eat something different?" He took some American cheese from his pocket.

One night Jurek discovered that Sasha was missing from their blanket. In the morning he asked, "Where were you last night?"

"I'll tell you someday."

"When?"

"When we get the order to move."

"To move where?"

"On to Germany."

"What about me?" Jurek asked.

"I'll think of something for you. Don't worry."

"But I want to come with you."

"You've already seen enough fighting. Remember those three German prisoners?"

Jurek remembered.

When winter came, he took his shoes from his knapsack and tried putting them on. To his surprise, they no longer fit him. Sasha brought a pair of army boots, stuffed them with paper, and laced them for him. Jurek was thrilled. Although the boots weren't new, they were in good condition and had studded soles. And when it snowed, Sasha brought him long army underwear and a heavy greatcoat.

"It's the smallest size I could find," he apologized.

"I don't need underwear," Jurek said, regarding the gift dubiously.

"Wear it. It will keep you warm. You can roll the tops down if it's too big. And there's a drawstring, see? Try it."

"Later," Jurek said.

Sasha put the coat on him, marked it like a tailor, and took in the waist and both sleeves. He hesitated before shortening the right sleeve. Even before Jurek could say anything, though, he cut it to the same length as the left sleeve.

"You can stick the end into your pocket," he said.

Jurek tried on the coat.

"It looks good," Sasha said. "Now peek through the window of the farmhouse and tell me if the Cherkas are sitting down to eat."

Jurek took a peek.

"Not yet."

"Tell me when they do."

When it was the family's suppertime, Jurek called Sasha. Sasha had a bottle of vodka.

"Come with me," he said.

He knocked on the door and they entered. Christina looked flustered. Her parents didn't know what to make of it. Pan Cherka saw the vodka and invited Sasha and Jurek to join them for supper. After grace, they all crossed themselves. The two grown-up men clinked glasses to toast the war's end and Hitler's death. They began to eat. Christina, blushing, sat by Jurek. She tried to help him to cut his food. Sasha said, "There's no need for that, Christina. He can manage by himself."

The two parents exchanged glances.

Sasha refilled the glasses. Now they drank a toast to Stalin and Mother Russia. Sasha poured some vodka for Jurek, but Jurek didn't want any. He had tried it once and it had burned his throat.

"To a free Poland!"

For the fourth toast, Sasha lifted his glass and said, "To Christina, the most beautiful girl in the world!"

He said to Jurek, "Tell them what I said."

Jurek translated.

This time the glances between Christina's parents were worried. Christina fled to the kitchen. Sasha said, "I've come to tell you that we're moving out."

Jurek was alarmed. "You are?"

"Just say what I ask you to."

Jurek waited for Christina to return from the kitchen.

"We're moving on to Berlin," Sasha said proudly.

They all understood that. He got to his feet and said grandly, "When the war is over, I'll return. With your permission, I want to marry Christina then."

Jurek translated.

Christina covered her face with her hands. There was a hush. Everyone held his breath and looked at her father.

"Do you agree to become a Catholic?" he asked.

"Yes," Sasha said.

That was that, then.

"We'll wait for you and pray for you," Pan Cherka said.

Pani Cherka clapped her hands with emotion.

"One more thing," said Sasha. "I want to leave the boy with you."

Jurek translated, embarrassed. Everyone looked at him.

"What's your name?" Pan Cherka asked.

"Jurek Staniak."

"Are you a Catholic?"

"Yes."

"Where did the Russians find you?"

"In the fields."

"You speak Russian well," Christina's mother said.

"I've been with them since last summer," Jurek told her.

There followed the usual questions about his parents, his village, and where he was during the war. He gave the usual answers.

"What can you do around a farm?"

"Everything—pasture the cows, tend the pigs, whatever you like."

"We'll take him," Pani Cherka said.

Pan Cherka nodded in agreement.

It was time to part. Sasha rose. Jurek rose to go with him.

"No," Sasha said. "You stay here."

Jurek was dumbfounded. "So soon?"

He sat down again. Sasha said goodbye to them all. He picked Jurek up and hugged him.

"You'll be fine here," he said. "These are good people."

"Would you like to eat something different?" Jurek asked.

Sasha was taken by surprise. He glanced at Jurek's clenched fist. Jurek opened it. In it was his cigarette lighter. For a moment, Sasha hesitated. Then he kissed Jurek and took the gift.

"I'll walk you," said Christina, putting on her fur coat.

"But it's snowing," Pani Cherka objected.

"It's all right," Pan Cherka said. "Just don't go far."

Sasha shook Pan Cherka's hand. Then he kissed Pani Cherka's hands, and he and Christina stepped outside. Her parents hurried to the window. Jurek was behind them. Snow was falling. The two young people walked arm in arm down the street. Sasha's comrades were preparing to move out. They cheered when they saw him with Christina. The two hugged and kissed and Christina ran back to the house, red as a beet.

"Isn't Sasha Catholic?" Jurek asked.

"No," Pani Cherka said. "The Russians are different."

Sasha didn't look any different.

"Is Berlin far?"

"Don't ask so many questions."

"It's very far," Christina sighed.

"Don't worry about it," Pani Cherka said. "He's only a Russian. Who knows what kind of home he comes from?"

"Mama!" Christina protested.

"First let's see if he comes back," Pan Cherka said.

16.

The War Is Really Over

In early spring of that year the Wisla overflowed its banks and flooded the entire region. Once the levees of the river were breached, there was nothing in the broad plain to stop the rampaging water, which rolled on for miles in all directions.

The cows in the barn began to bleat. Jan, the hired hand, woke up first. He jumped down from the hayrack on which he slept with Jurek and found himself in ankle-deep water.

"Jurek, wake up! There's a flood!"

From the stable came the frightened whinnies of the horses. The water had reached the animals' quarters first, because the farmhouse stood on a low rise.

Jurek groped in the darkness. Water was everywhere. "Where is it coming from?" he asked.

"The Wisla's overflowed. Go get the horses."

"The Wisla? It's far away."

"Don't talk now. Run! I'll get the cows."

Jurek waded through the water to the stable door. The horses were restless. They pawed at the water with their hooves as if they understood what was happening. He freed them and they bolted outside. Then he ran to the farmhouse, banged on the door, and shouted:

"Pan Cherka! There's a flood! There's a flood!"

A kerosene lamp shone yellow in the window. The door opened. Wojciech Cherka peered out and yelled, "Wife! There's a flood! Wake Christina!"

"The pigs!" shouted Pani Cherka.

Jan joined them, and they all splashed together to the pigsty. Everyone grabbed a piglet or two and brought it to the farmhouse. Oinking angrily, the mother sow trotted after them and ran into the house on their heels. Pan Cherka slammed the door. Water trickled through the cracks between the planks.

"Everyone up to the attic!" he ordered.

First they carried the piglets. Then they tried pushing the sow up the stairs. She balked and wouldn't move.

"Leave her alone," Pan Cherka said. "Bring up the furniture. She'll come by herself when the water gets high."

"What about the horses and cows?" Jurek asked Jan.

"When they have to, they'll swim. If they can find some high ground and keep from drowning, they'll come back. And don't ask so many questions, because Pan Cherka is going to smack you."

They began carrying things to the attic.

A gray, foggy morning found the sow floating in the downstairs room, half-propped on the stairs. The water had reached the windows. As soon as there was enough light to see, Jan and Pan Cherka pulled the sow up the stairs while Pani Cherka, Christina, and Jurek held her squealing piglets in the air to entice her. She oinked back at them and let herself be hauled to the safety of the attic.

The view from the attic window was like none Jurek

had seen. Only the top branches of the trees in the nearby woods were visible. Nothing remained of the houses but the roofs. The neighbors were worse off then the Cherkas. They sat on their roofs, clinging to the chimneys. Some held babies or piglets. The rain kept coming down.

In the afternoon, a rescue team of Polish soldiers arrived in rubber boats. Jurek was excited to see soldiers in Polish uniforms. For the first time he really believed the war was over. The soldiers helped the villagers down from the roofs. In the end, a boat reached their attic.

"We're staying here," Pan Cherka told the soldiers through the attic window. "Just take the boy. He's not ours and I don't want to be responsible for him."

He picked Jurek up and passed him through the window to a soldier.

The soldier squeezed Jurek into the crowded boat between babies and piglets. They cast off from the house. Jurek turned to say goodbye to the Cherkas. Christina stuck her head through the window and waved.

They motored over the vast flood, past inundated villages and treetops. No one spoke. Everyone had his own worries and tried not to move to keep the boat from tipping and filling with water. They headed for a section of the Wisla where the levees had held and moored in a little harbor. A soldier tied the boat, and they climbed carefully out of it onto a wet wooden dock. The soldiers took them to a church.

"Where are your parents?" a soldier asked Jurek.

"I don't have any."

"I have orders to bring all the orphans to a children's home."

Jurek shrugged.

"Wait here," the soldier said. "Maybe there are others."

Jurek was gone by the time the soldier returned. He wanted a real home, not an orphanage.

He was in Warsaw. It was a large city with apartment buildings and shops in its center and country houses and small farms on its outskirts. Jurek headed for the outskirts. Everywhere he saw burned-out ruins and blackened trees with broken branches. A charred tank lay in a ditch. In a suburb called Wawer he came to a small farm, entered the yard, and looked around. There were some auxiliary buildings and a wagon. A large oak tree spread its bare branches over the thatched roof of the farmhouse. Jurek liked the place and knocked. A middle-aged man opened the door. Jurek couldn't tell from the looks of him if he was a farmer, a hired hand, or some sort of tradesman.

"Blessed be Jesus Christ," he said.

"Forever and ever, amen," the man answered.

Jurek glanced inside. There was a large room with a big bed. A kerosene lamp stood on a table. By the lit stove a woman sat knitting. She looked up at Jurek without stopping her work. A boy his age was eating at the table.

"Are you one of the flood victims?" the man asked.

"Yes," Jurek said.

"Come in. I'll give you something to eat."

Jurek sat by the boy. The man brought him a plate of food. Jurek began to eat. Exhausted from his sleepless night, he felt his eyes beginning to shut.

"The boy needs to sleep," the woman said.

She rose, took a blanket from the closet, handed it to Jurek, and told her son, "Tadek, take the lamp and show the boy to the barn."

"And don't start any fires," his father said. "And come back right away, do you hear?"

Tadek took the lamp from the table and led Jurek to the barn. It was a small barn with only four cows. There was no hayrack. Tadek shone the light on a corner with some straw. Jurek spread his blanket. He was asleep before Tadek returned to the house.

Jurek stayed with the Kowalskis. Pan Kowalski was a blacksmith by trade. Mostly, he shoed horses. Apart from that, he had a small farm with a vegetable garden, two horses of his own, and some pigs and chickens. Now that much of Warsaw lay in ruins after heavy fighting, which ended with the Russian advance continuing, there weren't many horses to shoe. Pan Kowalski worked mainly at hauling loads in his wagon, such as debris to be cleared and bricks for rebuilding. Tadek and Jurek helped. Sometimes they went into town with him and sometimes they stayed behind to take care of the animals. The one thing they refused to do was go to school. Each time Pan Kowalski tried to make them, they ran away.

On one of their trips to the city, Pan Kowalski pointed at a burned-out neighborhood and said:

"That was the Jewish ghetto."

Jurek couldn't believe his eyes. Suddenly it all came back to him: the streets, the houses, his parents, the blurred figures of his brothers and sisters. It was all gone.

Every Sunday he went with his new family to church. In

the morning he washed in the horses' drinking trough, donned Tadek's second-best suit, and put on his Russian army boots.

One weekday morning, Tadek and his father went off in the wagon and Jurek stayed behind to help Pani Kowalski on the farm. Finishing his chores early, he went for a walk in the streets, hoping to find someone to play with. But all the children were in school, and after a while he found himself in front of a church. After a moment's deliberation, he entered. The church was empty, not the way it was on Sundays. There wasn't a sound. He sat down near the altar and looked around. A door creaked and a priest appeared. He was wearing an ordinary cassock, not the ornamented vestments used for mass.

"Playing hooky, eh?" the priest asked jokingly.

"No," Jurek said. "I was just passing by."

"Who are you?"

"I'm Jurek Staniak. I live with the Kowalskis."

"Oh, yes," the priest remembered. "You're one of the flood victims. Come, help me move a table."

He noticed Jurek's missing arm.

"Never mind," he said. "I'll do it myself."

Jurek was insulted. "I can do everything, Father."

The priest realized his mistake. He nodded and let Jurek help him carry a table to his room.

"Would you like some tea?" he asked.

"Yes, please."

The priest made tea and put a plate of cookies on the table. They both sat down.

"How old are you?"

Jurek thought.

162

"About ten."

"Have you been confirmed?"

Jurek knew what being confirmed was. He had seen boys and girls in the villages going to church for it. The girls looked like princesses in their white dresses and crowns of flowers, and even the toughest boys looked like gentlemen.

"No," he said.

"We're having confirmation for a large group of children soon. I'll speak to your adopting family."

Did that mean he would he look like those children? It was hard to believe.

Subsequently, he returned to the church several times. He dusted the objects in the sacristy, hoed the garden, sawed wood for the stove in the kitchen, and chatted with the priest over tea.

"How did you lose your arm?" the priest asked one day.

"It was caught in a machine. The lousy doctor didn't want to operate and left me all night in the corridor."

"Why didn't he want to?"

Jurek squirmed. "I don't know."

The priest said nothing for a while. Then he asked, "He didn't say anything?"

"I don't remember."

"But you were treated in the end?"

"The next day another doctor came. He had to amputate because I had gangrene."

Another time, the priest told Jurek he had been with the partisans during the war.

"Where?" Jurek asked.

"In the Kampinowki forest. For a whole year."

"I was there too," Jurek said, happy to tell about it. "Sometimes, in summer, I'd leave the farms I worked on and live in the forest."

"I once ran into some Jewish boys there," the priest said.

Jurek gave him an anxious look. But the priest's face was friendly. "Did you ever see any partisans?" he asked.

"Once. They shot my dog because a mad dog bit it."

Jurek told the priest about Azor. It made him sad.

✡

A large group of nine- and ten-year-olds was to be confirmed in May. Pan Kowalski grumbled that he would have to pay for private catechism lessons for Jurek and Tadek. The other children studied religion in school.

"Will you hire the priest?" his wife asked.

"Why the priest? I'll take a novice."

"We can pay him with a dozen eggs," Pani Kowalski said.

"Let it be a dozen eggs," Pan Kowalski agreed goodnaturedly. "As long he saves those two young sinners."

The two boys, freshly washed, combed, and dressed in their Sunday best, waited excitedly for the novice to come. A teenager, he talked to them at length about sin: which sins you went to hell for, and which you didn't, and how you could atone for them all by confession.

"And then you don't go to hell?"

"Once you've confessed, you're pure again," he promised them. "But you have to confess everything. If you don't, your soul stays filthy and nothing will help you."

There was one thing, Jurek knew, that he could not

164

possibly confess. But was being Jewish a sin? And if it was, did you go to hell for it? He prayed every night to Jesus and Mary and often touched the cross and the medallion of the Madonna that were always around his neck.

On the Saturday before confirmation, he and Tadek went to confession. Jurek had learned his lines by heart. He entered the confession box, crossed himself, and recited to the latticework partition that separated him from the priest:

"I have sinned the following sins against God. I have stolen chickens, eggs, vegetables, and fruit, and I once even stole a farmer's jacket."

He stopped. He could hear his father telling him, "Never forget that you're a Jew." But was that a sin? Did he have to confess to it? He went on: "If there were more sins that I don't remember, I'm sorry for them, too. I promise to mend my ways from now on."

When they came home for supper that night, the two boys were astonished to see two sets of freshly ironed white clothes—pants, shirts, jackets, and lace collars—and two new pairs of shiny shoes.

"Is that what we're wearing tomorrow?" Jurek asked.

"Yes," Pani Kowalski said. "In the morning I'll heat water and you'll wash well. I borrowed the clothes from the neighbors."

"I'll wash at the trough," Jurek said.

"You can't wash with soap at the trough," Pani Kowalski told him.

"You'll wash here, as you were told," Pan Kowalski ordered him sternly.

Jurek quailed.

"No one will see you, you silly boy," Pani Kowalski laughed. "We'll draw the curtain."

She showed Jurek a curtain that could be drawn to screen off the tub.

"Eat all you can tonight," Pan Kowalski advised. "Tomorrow morning you're not allowed to."

"Or to drink," his wife added.

The two boys sighed.

"For how long?"

"Until lunchtime, when the ceremony is over."

The next morning, a large piece of laundry soap was waiting for him on a stool by the tub. A bucket of hot water stood beside it.

"It's better than the trough," Pani Kowalski said, combing Tadek's washed hair. "Take off your clothes, stand in the tub, and wash yourself well. If there's any place you can't reach, Pan Kowalski will help you."

"I'll be fine," Jurek said.

"After you've dried yourself, put on your underwear and I'll help with the rest," Pani Kowalski said, handing Jurek an article of clothing he had never seen before.

"What's this?" he asked.

"Haven't you ever seen a pair of underpants?"

"Yes. The Russian soldiers gave me some last winter, to keep me warm. But those were long."

"Well, from now on you'll wear underpants all the time."

Jurek put on the underpants and stepped out from behind the curtain. He didn't know how to put on his new clothes, and Pani Kowalski helped him expertly into them.

Then she brushed and combed his hair vigorously. Last, she put on his lace collar and brought him to the mirror.

Jurek was dumbfounded. Another boy was standing there. But this boy, too, had only one arm.

The confirmation ceremony was impressive. All the boys held candles, and all the girls, white roses. The mass took longer than usual, and Jurek's stomach was rumbling from hunger. In the end, the children were called up to the altar for their first communion. Each knelt and was given a wafer. The small white cracker only made Jurek hungrier. He couldn't wait to go home and eat lunch.

17.

The Kidnappers

Jurek stayed with the Kowalskis a whole year. Gradually the hauling jobs diminished and Pan Kowalski went back to his smithy. Jurek was fascinated by everything about it—the fire, the bellows, the expertly delivered hammer blows that could turn a white-hot piece of iron into an ax, horseshoe, or sickle. Although Jurek taught himself to operate the bellows with one hand and a shoulder, the long tongs needed two hands, and so Pan Kowalski made him special one-handled tongs of his own. He learned to pluck the glowing iron from the fire with them and to lay it quickly on the anvil. Pan Kowalski showed him how to give it the desired shape by turning and pounding it.

Behind the house were fields. They were green in spring, yellow in summer, and snow-white when winter came. On winter days he joined the boys' snowball fights and in summer he went with Tadek to swim in the Wisla. Now that he had underpants, he no longer feared being seen naked. Not that they kept him from almost drowning the first time he tried to swim. Tadek had to pull him out of the water.

"Why didn't you tell me you couldn't swim?" he asked.

"I thought I could figure it out myself," Jurek answered.

Before long he learned to do a one-armed sidestroke.

Sometimes he went to the Wisla by himself, when the other boys weren't swimming or playing pranks in it. He liked to sit on the bank and watch the boats. There were barges and tugboats and sailboats that looked like white butterflies. Someday, he thought, he would own a sailboat and sail far, far away to the sea.

✡

One morning a taxi pulled up in front of the Kowalskis' house. Jurek, who was standing outside, went to have a look. Taxis were not a common sight in the neighborhood. An elegantly dressed man stepped out of it and asked for the Kowalski family.

"Right here," Jurek said.

"Are you Jerzy Staniak?"

"Yes."

The man introduced himself. He had a German-sounding name. Jurek thought he might be Jewish. He said, "I'd like to have a word with you. Get into the taxi for a minute."

He opened the door. Jurek hesitated. Something wasn't right. The taxi, which at first glance had made him curious, now seemed like a trap. He ran to the smithy and told Pan Kowalski, "Someone wants to kidnap me."

Pan Kowalski stepped outside with his hammer. The stranger introduced himself again. Pan Kowalski wiped a grimy hand on his work pants, and they shook hands.

"Can we talk in private?" the stranger asked.

"Of course," Pan Kowalski said, inviting him into the kitchen.

Jurek waited worriedly outside. A few minutes later he

was told to come in. The stranger said to him, "I'm a Jew. I've come from America. My whole family perished in the Warsaw ghetto. I was saved because I went to see the world's fair in New York and couldn't return because of the war." He made it sound like an apology. "I'd like to adopt you. You'll be well off with me."

"I'm not a Jew," Jurek said. He put his hand on his cross and medallion.

"I was given your name by a Jewish organization in Warsaw," the stranger went on. "You're on a list of Jewish orphans. I'll take you to America. I'll hire the best private tutors for you until you're ready to go to school. You'll lack for nothing."

"No," Jurek said. "I'm not a Jew."

"I'm sure you are. You strike me as a clever boy. The war taught you to hide your origins. You're still doing it now. But in the end you'll return to your roots. I'm ready to take you and look after you. I'll be your family."

"I have a family," Jurek said. "I don't want to go to school. I want to stay here."

The man said goodbye and left. The taxi drove away. A band of barefoot boys ran after it and waved. When it was gone Pan Kowalski said, "We could have made a lot of money, but we didn't want to sell you."

"He thought I was a Jew," Jurek said.

"Never mind," said Pani Kowalski. "Jesus was a Jew at first, too. As far as we're concerned, you've been confirmed and you're a Christian."

"You should know, though," Pan Kowalski put in, "that from now on the Jews will try to take you."

"Let them try," Jurek said. "They can't make me."

He couldn't say his prayers that night. He didn't know which sin was greater: betraying Jesus and the Holy Mother or betraying his promise to his father.

Two or three more Jews came to visit. These were young ones. They spoke about a children's home, school, new clothes, gym lessons, as if these were the things that could make him happy. The more they went into it, the more frightened he grew. Everything they offered him seemed like some kind of torture.

✡

One overcast autumn day, a small pickup truck drove up with two men in it. The cabin door opened and one got out. The driver remained inside. The man turned to Jurek and said, "Moshe Frankel."

Jurek knew at once what it was about.

"I'm not a Jew," he said. "And I'm not going anywhere with you."

Moshe Frankel tried to grab him, but Jurek was too quick. The man went off somewhere, leaving the truck and driver waiting. Jurek knew he'd be back.

"Tadek," he yelled. "Quick, bring the ladder!"

Tadek ran and brought the ladder and they stood it against the oak tree in the yard. Jurek filled his pockets with stones, climbed to a triple fork in the tree, and waited there tensely. Soon Moshe Frankel returned with a policeman. Jurek hadn't counted on that.

"Take away the ladder!" he told Tadek.

Frankel and the policeman entered the yard.

"Bring that ladder back," the policeman ordered Tadek.

Tadek refused. Meanwhile, the Kowalskis and some neighbors appeared on the scene. The policeman told Pan

Kowalski to bring the ladder. He brought it and leaned it against the tree.

"I'll brain anyone that comes near!" Jurek shouted from above, brandishing a stone.

Moshe Frankel believed him and kept his distance. He tried convincing Jurek to come down, to no avail. There was a brief consultation. The policeman slipped his rifle from his shoulder, cocked it, and fired a shot. Jurek was frightened and climbed down from the tree. Moshe Frankel seized him tightly.

"Pan Kowalski," Jurek called as he was being dragged off to the truck, "don't worry! I'll be back!"

He had hoped to be put in the back of the truck. But by now Moshe Frankel knew whom he was dealing with. He took out some rope, tied Jurek, put him in the cabin, and went to sit in the back himself.

The truck took them to Praga, the neighborhood of Warsaw on the Wisla's right bank, to a Jewish children's home on Jagielonska Street. Moshe Frankel waited for Jurek to climb down, untied him, and led him into an office. He locked the door and began to interrogate the boy.

"What's your name?"

"Jurek Staniak."

"That's impossible. You're a Jew."

"No, I'm not."

"Well, whoever you are, you smell bad and your clothes must be full of lice. You'll take a shower and then we'll talk."

Frankel summoned a teenager, who took Jurek to a

room with shiny white walls and a white tile floor as smooth as a church's. Along one wall was a row of sinks and faucets, with a mirror above each. Along the other wall was a series of glass partitions. Between every two partitions were pipes ending in what looked like the nozzle of a garden hose.

"What are those?" Jurek asked.

"You've never seen a shower?"

"No."

The boy sat him down, took out a hair clipper, and shaved Jurek's head. When he was done, he collected the hair and threw it in a bucket.

"That's to keep the lice from going for a walk," he said. "Now undress and throw your rags in here too."

He undressed. The boy opened two faucets between two partitions, tested the water, and told Jurek to stand under it. Jurek stuck out a hand and saw that it was hot. He would have stood there all day long had he been allowed to. But the boy shut off the faucets and told him to soap himself.

"Don't spare the soap," he said. "On your head, behind your ears, in all the hard-to-reach places. Between your toes, too. I have time."

It wasn't the usual big chunk of laundry soap but a round, slippery little bar that smelled of flowers. Each time it popped out of Jurek's hands, the boy bent down and picked it up. He turned the shower back on for Jurek to rinse himself, shut off the water, dried him with a large bath towel, took some fresh clothes from the closet, and offered to help him put them on.

"I can dress myself," Jurek said.

There were underpants, socks, pants, a shirt, a jacket, and brown shoes, all brand new.

"Try on the shoes. See if they fit."

They didn't. The boy brought him another pair. He watched, impressed, as Jurek laced the shoes with one hand. When Jurek was dressed, he brought him back to Moshe Frankel.

"He's Jewish, all right," he said and departed.

Moshe Frankel stepped up to Jurek. With a sudden movement he tore the cross and the medallion of the Madonna from his neck and threw them in the stove. Jurek gasped. He knew Frankel was stronger than he was.

"Some day I'll kill you," he said with helpless anger.

"I'm charmed," Moshe Frankel said. "You're not the first boy to tell me that."

He brought Jurek to a room with three beds. There was a locker next to each. Three chairs stood around a table. In the corner was a closet.

"This is where you'll live with two other boys," he said. He left and locked the door.

Bowls of candy and fruit lay on the table. Jurek ate an apple, slipped some candy into his pocket, and went to the window. The room was on the first floor and looked down at the yard below. Around the corner of the building, some children were playing soccer. Now and then one of them appeared chasing a real leather ball. Jurek tried opening the door. It stayed locked. He banged on it. No one came. He returned to the window, opened it wide, and leaned out. The drainpipe was almost within reach.

He stood on the windowsill, grabbed hold of the pipe, and slid down it with it between his legs. Then he went around the corner and asked to join the game.

"Are you the new boy?"

"Yes."

"You don't have an arm?"

"No."

"Show us."

"I don't feel like it. I have two legs."

After a brief debate over which team to put him on, Jurek joined the game. He let a few minutes go by and kicked the ball so hard that it flew over the fence.

The other boys were mad at him. "What kind of way is that to play? Now go get it."

That had been his intention all along. It was why he was playing in his new jacket.

"Help me over the fence," he said.

Two boys boosted him up and helped him reach the top. He jumped down on the other side, found the ball, kicked it back over the fence, and walked off. In the street he asked an old lady, "Excuse me, where is the train station?"

"It's not far from here," she told him.

She explained how to get there. Her explanation didn't help much because he couldn't read the street signs, but he found it in the end and asked for a train to Wawer. He was told how far to go, boarded the train, hid in the bathroom, counted three stops, and got off. To his surprise, he was in the right neighborhood. Whistling merrily, he walked to the Kowalskis. Pani Kowalski was home.

"Jurek!" She was happy to see him. "How nice you look! What clothes! Tadek and Pan Kowalski are in the smithy."

He raised a foot for her to see.

"And new shoes!"

They went together to the smithy.

"You see, Pan Kowalski," he said. "I told you I'd be back."

Pan Kowalski looked at him. "Those Jews have money. Why did they shave your head like a prisoner's?"

"That's how it is with them."

"You know they'll come to look for you."

"Sure. But you don't have to tell them I'm here."

He had no time to carry out his plan. Two policemen arrived to look for the blond, one-armed Jewish boy.

Jurek was taken back to the children's home.

18.

She Said Something
That Made Him Laugh

After breakfast in the dining hall, his two roommates went to school. Jurek was told to wait in the room.

"There's a lady who wants to talk to you," he was told.

Jurek was waiting for a chance to get away again. He didn't want any more questions. He had been asked enough of them. They were always the same. What was his name. Where was he from. What happened to his parents. Did he have brothers or sisters. He couldn't answer any of them and he was tired of them all. His name was Jurek Staniak. Yes, he knew he was Jewish. Yes, he had brother and sisters. How many? He didn't know.

There was a knock on the door. He put on his jacket and opened it. A gray-haired woman with a youthful face was standing there. She was not much taller than he was, and her glance met his directly. She had bright eyes and a friendly manner, and she shook his hand as though he were a grownup, letting go of it only when she had led him to a chair. She sat on his bed, facing him, and said something that made him laugh. Afterward, when he tried remembering what was so funny, he couldn't think of it.

But she brought a new feeling into the room, warm and bracing.

"My name is Pani Rappaport," she said.

"I'm Jurek Staniak. I guess you know that."

"I do."

She took his hand and stroked it. He didn't pull it away.

"Jurek," she said, "I meet lost children like you all the time. They don't know who their parents are, or where they came from before they wandered in the forests or the villages, or hid with kind people who protected them. We've found children in convents and in orphanages. Mostly girls. I suppose you know why that is."

"Yes."

"I know it's hard for you. I understand."

She kept talking in the same quiet, musical voice. He wasn't listening to the words. Their separate syllables ran together in a single, soft melody. The warmth of her hand spread through him and became a lump in his throat. He didn't know why his eyes filled with tears. She stroked his face. He was making strange, groaning sounds. It was as if something had opened inside of him, leaving him defenseless and exposed. He tried to close himself off again but couldn't. It was no longer in his control. Suddenly all the dams had burst. He was overcome by a feeling of helpless loss that flowed out of him with his tears. Pani Rappaport held his head and cried too. Then his head was in her lap and he was talking. He told her everything he remembered, everything he had forgotten.

"Do you remember your name now?"

"No."

"You had brothers and sisters, didn't you?"

"Yes. But I can't remember their names, either."

"Do you remember where you're from?"

He suddenly recalled the name of the town. He could picture the bakery and his father standing in the glow of the oven. There had been a smithy next to it, and then their home, and Pani Staniak's little grocery across the street. And now he saw his grandfather with a long, white beard, and his mother. He strained to make out her face. He thought he caught sight of his brothers and sisters, too, although they remained hidden in darkness. He remembered his father lying in bed, snoring with a funny sound like a train whistle's. And himself climbing onto the bed and tickling his father's mustache with a plant stem. Then the face was gray and covered by stubble. They were in a potato field. His father's eyes burned into him. He could feel his breath and hear him saying, "You have to stay alive, Jurek." That wasn't the name he had been called. But he had stayed alive. It was in order to stay alive that he had forgotten his name and the names of his brothers and sisters and even the name of his mother. It had all vanished into the great emptiness that opened inside him on the day she disappeared.

Jurek wiped away his tears. In bits and pieces he tried telling Pani Rappaport about the scenes flashing through his mind.

"You say the town was called Blonie? Would you recognize it?"

"Yes," he said. "I'd recognize our house and the bakery. There was a smithy next to it."

"Would you go with me there now?"

They went in the little pickup truck in which he had

been kidnapped. The two of them squeezed into the cabin beside the driver. Pani Rappaport put her arm around him, but perhaps this was only because she had nowhere else to put it. Sitting so close to her gave Jurek a warm feeling. "You see," he joked, "there are good things about having only one arm."

She didn't laugh. She just gave him a big hug.

They crossed the Wisla. It took over an hour to reach Blonie. Little farms with thatched roofs stood on its outskirts. As they neared its center, these changed to low wood and brick houses. Suddenly Jurek shouted, "There's the bakery!"

The truck stopped. The door of the bakery was locked. Jurek ran to the smithy. No one was there, either. The place looked deserted. He grabbed Pani Rappaport's hand and pulled her after him. Soon they were standing in front of a half-destroyed house.

"This is where we lived," he said with a sinking heart.

He glanced across the street and his face lit up. "Pani Staniak's grocery is open!" he cried, pulling her after him again.

They entered the grocery. A middle-aged woman was standing behind the counter. She looked at Jurek wide-eyed and let out a cry.

"Srulik!"

Pani Staniak turned pale. She clutched at her heart and leaned against the counter.

"Srulik, you're alive?"

Now he remembered. Yes, his name was Srulik. Not Jurek Staniak.

Pani Staniak recovered, shut the store, and took the two

of them home with her. She served them tea and cookies and they sat around the table.

"Your mother and your brother Duvid were shot on the road not far from here," she told Jurek.

"Do you know Srulik's family name?" Pani Rappaport asked.

"Of course. You might as well ask if I know my own name. It was Frydman. He doesn't remember it?"

"No. He goes by the name of Jurek Staniak."

Pani Staniak laughed.

"Who gave you that name?"

"Papa."

"He wanted you to have one you could remember. I knew the whole family well," she said to Pani Rappaport. "We were good neighbors. We were once invited to their Passover Seder and they came to see us celebrate our holidays. Srulik, don't you remember our Christmas tree?"

Srulik grinned. He remembered. The grin was for what happened when he came back from looking at the Christian tree with its little candles and stars. His parents weren't home, and his brother took a hammer and hit him on the head.

"Your big sister was Feyge. She escaped to Russia with your uncle when the war broke out. Your other sister was Malka. Your brothers were Yoysef and Duvid. You were little Srulik."

Pani Staniak smiled at him.

"What were the names of Srulik's parents?" Pani Rappaport inquired.

"His father was Hersh and his mother was Riva. She was a pretty woman."

Jurek tried picturing his mother again. He still couldn't do it. He could see his father more clearly. Not the haggard, stubbly face in the potato field, but his real one.

They said goodbye to Pani Staniak. She kissed Jurek and shook Pani Rappaport's hand. On their way to the truck, Pani Rappaport hugged him and said, "Now we'll look for your sister Feyge."

"All right," he said. "But I want to go on being Jurek."

"Then you will be," she promised.

On the return trip to Warsaw, Jurek was preoccupied with his thoughts. More and more memories kept occurring. Of someone swinging a chicken above his head. Of cleaning the house for a holiday and taking out all the mattresses and filling them with new straw. He remembered where each bed had stood, the one he shared with Duvid too. He remembered the corner for washing—or was he thinking of the Kowalskis'? He remembered the bucket that stood on the porch on winter nights, so that they needn't go all the way to the wooden outhouse. He remembered his grandfather taking him to the stuttering hatter and buying him a hat with a button on top. He could picture the pantry with its double doors and the drawers beneath them, in one of which his mother kept the cakes she baked. The memories kept coming, as though in a strange dream.

"Jurek, wake up."

His mother was bending over him. He knew it was a dream and that the voice was Pani Rappaport's. And yet it was his mother, too, her face as clear as if she were standing there. He did everything not to let go of her. He would never forget her again.

"We're here," Pani Rappaport said.

He opened his eyes. He could remember his mother.

✡

Jurek was excited and nervous when he went the next week to say goodbye to the Kowalskis. Hearing the hammer from the smithy, he went there first.

"I've come to say goodbye," he said.

Pan Kowalski went on shaping a piece of iron. Tadek glanced at him and resumed working. Jurek waited.

Pani Kowalski saw Jurek through the window and came from the house. Pan Kowalski put down his hammer and wiped his hands. Then he wiped his brow.

"He's come to say goodbye," Tadek told his mother.

Jurek gulped and said, "I'm staying on in the Jewish children's home."

"It's up to you," Pan Kowalski said.

"God watch over you," said Pani Kowalski, kissing him on his head.

"It's the same God as ours," Pan Kowalski said.

Jurek put his hand in his shirt and felt his neck. There was nothing there.

Pan Kowalski gave him a left-handed handshake.

Tadek walked him to the train station. He couldn't read, either. They had to ask directions. Jurek bought a ticket to Warsaw. The platform was crowded with passengers. When the train arrived, he pushed his way to a window. Tadek was standing on the platform. He grinned at Jurek. Jurek grinned back.

Epilogue

Pani Rappaport searched Polish government lists of returnees from Russia after the war. She discovered that Pani Fayge Frydman had come back to Poland and left again for an unknown destination. A few years later, a staff member at the children's home moved to Israel and promised Jurek to look there for his sister. She turned to the missing persons' bureau and found her. Jurek received a letter from Fayge, with photographs of her, her husband, and their two Israeli children. By then he had learned to read.

From Warsaw he was transferred to a children's home in the city of Lodz. He finished the eight years of elementary school in four years and the four years of high school in two years and continued at a local university. At first he thought of majoring in Polish history and Marxism, but his old high school adviser talked him out of it. "Are you crazy?" he said angrily. "What do you need all that Communist nonsense for? What will you do with it if you also decide to move to Israel some day? You're good at mathematics. Study that."

Jurek took his advice. He lived in the dorms and received a double fellowship, once as a war invalid and once as an outstanding student.

One Saturday night he took a trolley with a friend to a student function. Suddenly, looking out the window, he saw a beautiful girl in a red coat. Without thinking twice, he jumped from the moving trolley and followed her. Although after a while she felt she was being trailed, she was afraid to turn around. She entered the building of the Jewish Students Club and climbed some stairs. Jurek climbed behind her. On the door was a note saying, "We've all gone to the theater."

Frightened, she turned around and saw Jurek, the blond, one-armed Jewish student renowned for being one of the most eligible young men on campus.

Her name was Sonia. Despite the love that blossomed between them, they were forced to part a year later when her family moved to Israel. Yet they kept writing to each other.

Jurek graduated and found work as an assistant teacher in the Polytechnic Institute. After encountering more than one incident of anti-Semitism, he decided to leave for Israel, too. There he was reunited with his sister and her family, and he married Sonia. They had two children, a son and a daughter.

In Israel, Jurek took the Hebrew name of Yoram. He went on teaching mathematics and also taught others to teach it.

In both Poland and Israel, he declined to be fitted with a prosthesis. He had gotten along with one arm as a boy, he said, and could do everything with it now, too—even wash the dishes.

During his first years in Israel, he told the story of his years in wartime Poland to many people, all of whom thought he was exaggerating. A few years after the 1973 Yom Kippur War, the school he taught in was visited by a guest speaker, a man who had lost an arm and both legs in the fighting yet managed to go on living an active life. At the end of his talk, Yoram rose and told his story again. This time, to his surprise, the audience was enthralled. You could have heard a pin drop. Many people were moved to tears.

As was I when I heard it.

Uri Orlev
Jerusalem, 2000